SIGNS OF AFFECTION

SIGNS OF AFFECTION

ESKAY KABBA

4 Horsemen
Publications, Inc.

DEDICATION

To Eric T., for always believing in my talent. Connor is alive because of you.

And to all the CJ's out there. Everyone needs a CJ in their life, if only for a moment.

CONTENTS

Chapter 1 What do you want to know? 1
Chapter 2 He's A Lucky Man 20
Chapter 3 That's Not Donny 40
Chapter 4 Big Daddy 55
Chapter 5 He's Your Goddamn Son 70
Chapter 6 My Family Is Already
    Being Torn Apart 81
Chapter 7 I'm Here To Support Connor 98
Chapter 8 Merchant Is a Dick.. 121
Chapter 9 Tell Us About That.. 140
Chapter 10 Honesty, Acceptance
    and Forgiveness 161
Chapter 11 Nothing Will Ever Be the Same 176
Chapter 12 Sloppy 193
Chapter 13 Not My Circus,
    Not My Monkeys 211
Chapter 14 That's Pride 221
Epilogue 243

Book Club Questions 251
Author Bio: 253

CHAPTER 1

"WHAT DO YOU WANT TO KNOW?"

If someone would have told me three years ago that I would be sitting in a jail cell waiting to be arraigned for attempted murder, I would have laughed. I do crazy shit, but not *that* crazy. However, if they would have told me who in fact I attempted to murder… I might have believed it. I mean, really, isn't that why I went into the Marine Corps in the first place, to learn how to kill the abusive fuck that just happened to be my father?

~~~July 2012 ~~~

The sun hadn't even risen when the cops banged on our door. Jamel and I both woke with a start, sitting up and staring into the darkness. I reached out for him, and he must have known because he instantly caught my waving hand. We squeezed hands tightly, but he let me go first and started putting on clothes.

I told him, "It's gonna be fine because I'm going with you."
~~~

Jamel shook his head as he threw his t-shirt on. "Just call my dad. He has a friend who's a criminal lawyer in Providence. He'll know what to do. Meet me there later."

We went downstairs and I watched him put on his sneakers. The police continued to bang on the door. I called out, "Hold on a fucking minute!"

I probably sounded angrier than I should have, but I was scared. I was scared that they were going to put Jamel, my black partner, in jail for what *I* did. With his gun.

He's fucked, and it's all my fault.

Jamel kissed me passionately, holding me by the back of my neck and pulling my thin bottom lip between his two bigger ones. He rubbed my nose with his, then rested his cheek on mine. "It will be fine, Connor. We're going to cooperate," he said in my ear.

I couldn't speak, a lump forming in my throat. All I could think about was how unfair it was that another person I loved was going to be forced to leave me. My heart was shattering moment by moment.

He abruptly let me go and went to answer the door while I stayed near the stairs. He opened it and a man dressed in a long, brown trench coat paused mid-knock. He was straight out of a TV cop show with his white pinstriped shirt, tan pants, scuffed shoes, and clashing blue tie. He looked startled to see Jamel: a dark brown skinned, 6'2 solid body mass of a man with gray eyes. He almost took a step back; the guy had to be half Jamel's size. But then I guess he remembered that he was the one with the badge and a gun.

Jamel was ready to step out of the doorway when the man asked, "Is Corporal Connor McIntyre on the premises?"

Jamel looked down at him, his brow furrowed. Curiosity got the better of me as well, so I walked over and stood behind him. "I'm Connor," I said hesitantly.

The man nodded. "We have a warrant for your arrest." He motioned for the officers behind him to grab me.

I instinctively took a step back as the two men came toward me, but then stood my ground. Jamel's mouth opened slightly, at a loss for words. In shock, I allowed them to put my arms behind my back and put the handcuffs on me. I only had on a tank top, sweat-shorts, and socks.

Jamel, mouth still opened, stepped to the side and allowed them to read me my rights and take me through the threshold of the door. But then he asked, "What's the charge?"

The man in the trench coat turned back. "Attempted murder."

Jamel's mouth opened wider and so did mine. We had this all wrong.

We thought that my racist, homophobic father would use their fight as an opportunity to get Jamel arrested on some bullshit assault charge. We took pictures of his face the night before: the black eye, his busted lip, and the scratches on his neck from when my father tried to choke him. We were ready to face whatever charges he was going to throw at us. But attempted murder? Unless he was a mind reader, that was a reach.

But I guess not because I'm the one being dragged out of the house toward the police vehicle at 3am, I thought.

Jamel, who rarely raises his voice, spoke loudly and angrily, "Attempted murder? Are you fucking serious!? If Connor wanted to kill him, he would have! It was self-defense."

His voice carried over to the street, and I wondered how many of our neighbors were looking out their windows at the three squad cars, their blue and red flashing lights lighting up our quiet one-way street. We're already an interracial, gay couple, so we were careful to avoid any unwanted attention in the last year we'd lived here. *So much for being inconspicuous. That shit went right out of the window today.*

I looked back as the officer had stepped into the house, gesturing at something inside. I knew exactly what he was pointing at: the huge blood stain left on my pewter blue loveseat near the door. The one Owen fell against when I shot him.

"Step aside, sir," I heard Trench Coat instruct Jamel, and four other officers walked into the home, probably to comb for more evidence.

The officers that held me were nice enough. They were both young-looking, older than 20 but not quite 30. They opened the car door and gently guided me inside by the back of my head. The door closed, and I looked out the window to see police swarming into my house. A light had been turned on.

Jamel ran out of the house with my Nike slippers in his hand. When he got close, one of the officers tried to stop him, but he yelled, "I just wanna—" I watched him take a step back, close his eyes, take a deep breath, and open them. He said very calmly, "I just want to talk to him. That's all. Just let me talk to him, please."

One of the officers gently touched his partner's arm and nodded, letting him know it was okay to step out of his way. "Five minutes," he said. He took the shoes from Jamel first.

Jamel knelt down so he could peer into the window. "Connor." The glass muffled his voice. "Connor, baby, you're gonna be okay. Okay?"

I love when he calls me baby. I used to laugh at couples that had pet names like "baby," "sweetie," and "love" for their significant others. It just sounded so corny. Even couples that said I love you every day seemed corny to me. But when Jamel called me baby, it made my heart go all mushy. And I was feeling corny.

"I love you," I murmured as I looked at him. My was heart full, despite the circumstances.

"I love you too," he said quickly, then continued reassuring me. "I'm going to call my dad right now. The plan is still the same. You won't stay in there. We're going to get you out and bring you home. Okay, baby?"

I gave him a small smile. "I love you," I said again.

His tough exterior cracked, and I caught the worry on his face. He placed his palm on the glass, and I shifted so I could put my forehead against it.

"That's enough," the officer who didn't want to allow this in the first place barked. He grabbed Jamel's arm.

Jamel wrenched his arm away and rose to his feet. "Get the fuck off me!" he snarled at the cop and got in his face.

The second cop, who had momentarily been kind, remembered that he was indeed a police officer and pulled his gun out, aiming it at my partner. "Back up, now! Or you'll be arrested too."

I had never seen Jamel get aggressive like that with anyone, let alone someone of authority. I knew that being gunned down by the police was his greatest fear, but the fear of losing me must have been greater. I had to make him stop. Because the last thing we needed was for both of us to end up in matching cells.

"Jamel! Jamel, fuck!" I yelled. "Calm the fuck down! Get back! Now! That's a fucking order, Sergeant! Get back now!"

He heard me. He raised his hands high in the air and took a large step back. He kept walking backwards, keeping his eyes on the officers. When his heel hit the bottom of our concrete step, he made the "I" in sign language, brought it to the center of his chest and rubbed it in a circular motion a couple of times before lifting his hand again. The officers probably thought it was weird, but I knew what it meant. Jamel has a tattoo of my initials on the inside of his right wrist; when he put it to his heart, it was his way of telling me that he loved me, no matter who was around or where we were.

I yelled from inside the vehicle, "I love you too, Mel!"

I'm sure he didn't hear me, but he saw my mouth move. My eyes watered and I couldn't help the tears from streaming down my face. Jamel kept his hands up but turned around to go back into the house. Because I was handcuffed, I couldn't wipe away my tears. I brushed my damp cheek against my shoulder, then

I turned away and faced forward. I didn't look at the house again, and he didn't come out either.

❤

After about 20 minutes, the two officers got in the car and took me not to the local police station in West Warwick, the township that we live in, but all the way to downtown Providence. They brought me into a room, and I sat there for another 30 minutes, handcuffed to a desk. At least they were nice enough to put my slippers on.

Trench Coat finally came in. "Corporal Connor McIntyre? I'm Detective Robert Gram. Sorry I didn't introduce myself earlier."

I kept my face stoic and didn't respond. He sat down at the table across from me and folded his hands. "So, it sounds like there was an altercation at your house earlier this evening. Do you want to tell me about it?"

I eyed him in silence.

He continued to speak in a soothing voice, like he was a fucking therapist and not the cop that just arrested me. "Your father was pretty banged up when he came into the hospital today. He's going to need surgery for that arm. He's making some pretty wild accusations about you. Can you tell me what happened?"

I blinked.

He sighed deeply. "Listen, son—"

"Don't call me son," I said abruptly.

He nodded. "I apologize, Corporal, I meant no disrespect. And thank you for your service, by the way. It must not have been easy over there, but I'm glad you found your way home. Many people don't. And if they do, they suffer from PTSD. Anger issues. Impulsivity. Explosive behaviors. Do you know what I mean, Corporal?"

He can't be serious right now. I'm over this "talk."

He tried again to ask, "Corporal, I'm just trying to understand what hap—"

"Has my lawyer arrived?" I asked curtly.

He looked surprised. "Are you requesting a lawyer?"

"I don't need to request a lawyer from you. Mine is already on his way. Unless he's already here. Is he here?"

"No, but—"

"Then we can talk when my lawyer gets here. Thanks." I glared at him.

He glared back at me, his understanding eyes not so understanding anymore. Then he looked at the two-way glass and nodded. An officer came in, the same one that let Jamel come close to the car. "Drop him in the tank," Trench Coat said coldly.

The officer raised both eyebrows, but he unlocked me from the desk and lifted me up by my arm. He led me downstairs to a large cell that had at least 15 other men in it. All of the benches were full. The gate closed behind me, and I put my hands through the slot so that the cuffs could come off. I surveyed the room first, getting a couple of hard looks from a few guys. I kept my face unreadable and found a wall to stand on. I slid down to sit on the floor with my knees up. The room was cold and the floor was colder, but I'd trained under worse circumstances with more dangerous men. I waited.

❤

Almost two hours later, the same officer called my name. "McIntyre!"

I stood up, my legs achy from being in the same position for so long, and walked over to the gate. "Hold out your wrists," the young man demanded. I did as he asked, and he put cuffs on me, then opened the bars to let me out.

"You must be a bad motherfucker," the guy closest to the bars said to me amusingly. I turned around and winked at him.

I was led back to that same interrogation room, but this time, there were two black men inside. I was relieved to see Major Wendel Jones, Jamel's father. He gently touched my face. "You okay, son?"

I nodded, a small lump forming in my throat from the Major calling me "son." At least I belonged to someone. He turned back to the table. "Jamel brought you clothes. He's waiting out front."

"Hey! Get these cuffs off him, now," the other man barked at the officer, who loitered in the doorway.

The cop hesitated. "I'm sorry, I can't do that. Detective's orders—"

"Has he shown any violent behaviors since the moment you read him his rights? Any resistance? Anything at all to indicate that he is a danger to anyone in this entire building?" The man scoffed. "No? Then get these cuffs off my client, or so help me God I will rain fire down on this rinky-dink operation you have going on here!"

Ah. This must be my lawyer.

The young officer hesitated again, but then he came over to me. I held out my wrists, and he unlocked the cuffs. "Thank you," I said quietly.

He nodded and looked into my eyes a little longer than he should have. I let the corners of my mouth turn up into a smile, letting him know I knew his secret. He practically ran out the room with fear in his eyes. I couldn't help but chuckle. Before Jamel, I would have had a pretty young thing like him face down in my bed before the night was over. But Jamel changed me for the better. Now, there was only one man I wanted in my bed.

My lawyer stepped out, and I heard the blinds rustle from the other side of the two-way mirror. "Privacy should be a thing around here," he said in a commanding voice. Then he came back into the room and closed the door.

"Thank you," I said.

"No problem." He held out his hand and I shook it. "I'm Lirion Kelly, defense attorney and retired Army Specialist. Get dressed, Corporal. It's going to be a long day."

I put on the jeans and long-sleeved t-shirt that Jamel sent over, then sat to tie my sneakers. Kelly took off his suit jacket and sat down, pulling out a notebook. The Major sat on the other side of me. After about ten minutes of watching him read, I got the feeling we were stalling out the detective.

Every once in a while, Kelly would look up and ask me a question that would start off with, "Just to confirm…" It sounded like Jamel told him about the history between my father and me, even the stuff that nobody else knew.

We were there for close to an hour before he finally turned to me. "Okay Connor, just tell them what happened, facts only. Not what you thought or were thinking. More like, what you were feeling. Facts or feelings only. If I tell you, 'Don't answer that,' you don't answer it. Got it?"

I nodded. "Yes, sir."

"You're ready?"

"Yes, sir."

"Good. Let's begin."

As Kelly walked over to the door to let the cops in the interrogation room, I had to stop myself from tapping my foot in nervousness. When we devised the game plan, Jamel said his father had connections with a law firm and that made me confident at the time. But now that I was the one on this side of the table, I didn't feel so confident. I looked over at the Major. He caught my eye and gave me one nod. I nodded back. His face was calm and that reassured me a little.

"Detective? We're ready," Kelly called out.

Trench Coat came into the room, but he was not alone. Another man followed him. He looked like an older version of me: blond hair, light blue eyes, but with the rugged physique of a model. I'm cute, but not cute enough to walk a runway. That guy could walk a runway. He was impeccably dressed like he was going on a dinner date, wearing a full suit, complete with vest and tie.

They sat down across from us. I felt Kelly tense next to me; he was clearly not happy about the second man's presence at all. Gram introduced him. "Corporal, this is ADA Alexander Merchant. He's here to evaluate whether or not this ends here or goes to trial."

"Trial?" Kelly boomed. "Aren't you getting ahead of yourself, Alex?"

"Not if he intended to kill his father," Merchant said factually. He turned to me. "Did you intend to kill your father, Connor?"

"Don't answer that!" Kelly said loudly. I wasn't going to anyway.

Merchant ignored him, keeping his eyes on me. "Connor," he said, "we're all just trying to figure out what happened tonight. You're facing some very serious charges. I'm not going to sugarcoat that for you. Now that your lawyer is here, let's lay everything out on the table. As long as you're honest, I can do what I can to help you here. But I need you to be honest."

I nodded. "What do you want to know?"

"Start from the beginning," Gram urged.

I gave Barney Fife a look. "The beginning of my life or the beginning of the night?"

He didn't like my snark, but Merchant seemed fine with it. "Tonight," he replied smoothly. "Well, last night actually." He looked at his watch. It was an expensive watch. "It's after 6 a.m. now. What happened last night?"

I looked at Kelly and he nodded. "Jamel and I were sitting down for dinner, and someone banged on the door. I was closest, so I opened it. My father, Owen, was there. He reeked of alcohol. He grabbed me by my shirt collar, cutting off my air, and told me to stop this gay shit and get in the car. He said that he was taking me home."

Merchant cut me off. "What did he mean by 'stop this gay shit'"?

"Don't answer that," Kelly said to me. He asked Merchant, "How would Connor know what his father meant?"

I could tell that the ADA was losing patience with my attorney. He rephrased the question. "Did he not know you were gay?"

I looked at my lawyer who nodded slightly. "No, he just found out last month. I told my parents and two of my three siblings six weeks ago."

Merchant nodded. "Okay, then what happened?"

I hesitated but decided to be honest. "Jamel came over, grabbed his arm, and gave him one warning: if he did not let me go, he was going to break his arm."

Merchant's eyes went wide. "So, Jamel was being aggressive."

"I didn't say tha—"

"No," Kelly cut in. "Jamel was being protective of his partner. No jury would see that as aggression, not when Owen struck first. Try again, Alex."

Merchant hardly glanced at him. "What happened next, Connor?"

"Owen let me go and pushed me, then he pushed Jamel. He called me a worthless piece of shit and started yelling that I was trying to take his girls away from him, my mom and my sisters. He was going to take me home and give me what I'm good for. Said some other nasty things I don't remember. Jamel stood between us and told him that I wasn't going anywhere, that if I wanted to be with him in his home, I would be. That it's my choice to be with him."

"And is it?" Merchant asked gently. "You don't feel coerced or manipulated into this relationship with Jamel Jones?"

"Oh, come on!" Kelly yelled at the same time the Major spoke for the first time, saying, "Is that a joke?"

Merchant leaned back in his chair. "I'm asking a legitimate question. Because the other side to this is that you, Connor, are being manipulated into an abusive, controlling, same-sex relationship that you don't necessarily want. That your father was just trying to help you get out of it, and you turned on him."

"That reeks of bullshit and you know it, Alex," Kelly scoffed.

"I'm just doing my job, Lirion. Asking the hard questions." He rested his elbows on the table and used his gentle voice again. "You're in a safe space. You can tell us the truth here."

Actually, no. If I was in an abusive relationship with Jamel, I couldn't say so because his father was sitting right next to me. So already the cops were doing a shit job at protecting me. But luckily, my situation was the complete opposite of the tale told by my father.

"The only abusive relationship I was in was one with my father, Staff Sergeant Owen McIntyre." I spoke clearly because I knew this was being recorded somewhere. "My father has physically, mentally, verbally, and emotionally abused me, my mother, and my siblings our entire lives. I went into the Marine Corps at 18 to escape his abuse. I came back four and half years later and the abuse continued. So, I moved out, distanced myself from him, and never looked back." I let my words hang in the air before I continued.

"Also, for the record, I'm in love with Sergeant Jamel Jones. I'm not being coerced or forced into loving him. I just do. And I plan to spend the rest of my life with him. That's why we bought a house together, to share our lives together. He has never put his hands on me or even said a negative word to or about me. He has never even raised his voice. And if you knew Jamel's personality, you would know that he doesn't raise his voice at anyone. He's the gentlest man I've ever met. He's loving, caring, and yes, protective over me, just like I am to him. We've been in love for almost three years, but my father just found out that we were more than friends a few weeks ago. That's what made him angry."

"That was beautiful, thank you." I could hear the sarcasm in the ADA's voice. I glared at him. "Other than the initial grab on your shirt, did your father actually strike you at any point?"

"No, Jamel wouldn't let that happen."

"Jamel got between the two of you?"

"Yes."

"And then what happened?"

"They started arguing about who was going to keep me—"

He cut me off. "What do you mean by, 'keep you'?"

"Sorry, that was the wrong choice of words. I mean, my father was saying stuff like, 'I'll kill you dead before I let a nigger like you have my son.' And Jamel was saying that I was already taken by him—"

"So, he *was* possessive over you?" Gram asked.

"No, no, that's not what I meant." I was getting flustered, so Kelly stepped in.

"Don't try to twist his words around," he snapped. "Obviously, Owen came there to essentially kidnap his own son and try to force him back home. Jamel was not going to allow that to happen, is that right?"

I was grateful for him. "Yes, that's right. Owen made it clear that he was there to make me go back home. And Jamel told him I already was home. So the arguing was around that."

"What happened next?" Merchant prompted.

"Owen got in Jamel's face. He tried to go around Jamel to get to me and Jamel pushed him back."

"So again, Jamel was the aggressor?" the ADA asked.

"I didn't say that." *I'm getting annoyed with this guy.*

"Again," Kelly reiterated, "it sounds like Jamel was protecting his partner from his abusive father. You call that aggression; I call that defense of his home and his family."

Merchant gave him a look of annoyance, then turned back to me. "Who struck first?"

"Owen," I said automatically. "Owen definitely swung first and hit Jamel in the face. Jamel swung back and they started fighting."

"Wait, what were you doing while all of this was happening?" Gram asked.

I froze for a moment. "I… I just stood there."

"You just stood there and let your boyfriend and your father square up and pummel each other?" Gram sounded unconvinced.

"I...." I didn't know what to say. *Do I tell them I had a flashback in the middle of all this?*

I glanced at Kelly and he must have seen it in my eyes. "Tell them how you were feeling," he murmured.

"I…" I turned back to Gram and Merchant. "I was scared. I was … kinda stuck."

"C'mon," Gram said. "You can't expect us to believe that you, a *Marine*, were afraid of your father."

"Have you ever been in an abusive relationship, Gram?" Kelly asked him. "Or at the very least, talked to anyone that has been? Or taken part in a domestic violence investigation?"

Gram shrugged dismissively. "I leave that to Special Victims. And those are mostly women."

"So, boys are never physically abused by their fathers? Grown men are never afraid of other grown men? Is that your professional assessment, detective?" Kelly asked nastily.

"I'm just saying," Gram said, getting louder. "He's not a boy; he's a man. He's a Marine, and he's trying to tell us he was afraid? What does he have to be afraid of?"

I blurted out, "I was afraid he was going to take me back to the basement."

"The basement?" Merchant looked confused.

"That's where the real beat downs happen. If he took you to the basement, you were going to end up in the hospital. For sure." I started trembling a bit. It was the first time I'd said it out loud in my 28 years on this Earth.

Merchant and Gram looked at each other and then at me. I tried to hold their gaze, but I averted my eyes out of shame and embarrassment. I felt the Major put his hand on my shoulder and squeeze.

It was deadly quiet until Kelly softly spoke. "Tell them the rest, Connor." I nodded, then turned my attention back to the cop and the ADA.

"They were fighting and Owen got the upper hand somehow. He wrapped his arm around Jamel's neck and started choking him. And I knew, I *knew* he was not going to let him go. He was going to kill Jamel right in front of me, force me back home, and beat the shit out of me. Or more likely, beat me to death right then and there. Because, in his eyes, gay people deserve to die the Old Testament way, with beatings and stoning. I couldn't let that happen. So I went for the gun that we keep locked in the safe. I grabbed Jamel's Sig because his was loaded and mine was not, and I fired once at Owen's right shoulder, just to make him let go. He fell backward off of Jamel, and I grabbed Jamel to stand closer to me. I said a couple of words about how he's a bully, a terrible husband and father, and an abusive fuck. I did tell him that he deserved to die for all of it. But I didn't fire the weapon to kill him. I could have, but I didn't. I wasn't trying to kill him. I just wanted him to leave me the fuck alone."

It was still quiet, so I continued. "Jamel took the gun from my hand and told Owen that if he ever trespasses in our home again, we will invoke Stand Your Ground and shoot him. Owen left after that, holding onto his bleeding shoulder."

Kelly took the opportunity to put his briefcase on the table and open it. He pulled out a clear Ziplock bag with the Sig and the shell casing inside. Hopefully, the bullet was still sitting in Owen's deltoid where I'd left it.

"Here is the weapon in question. I know the offi-cers were looking for it. You could have just asked nicely, and Jamel would have given it to you. It was in the safe in the dining room." Gram took the gun from him. "So are we done here, gentlemen?" Kelly asked.

Merchant stood up and took off his suit jacket. "We're just getting started."

HE'S A LUCKY MAN

They asked me a million questions, starting with the abuse I endured growing up. I told them about every single time I took a trip to the emergency room in the last 28 years and how every single instance was because of Owen. I told them about the time my brother Matthew was almost beaten to death by my father at 16, but lied to everyone about it when BJ brought him to Providence General Hospital. I told them to look up my mother's hospital records too. I was sure there was a record of her abuse somewhere.

They asked me about my previous relationships with men and women. I explained to them that I didn't suddenly become gay because of Jamel. I was bisexual in high school but dated men exclusively after I retired from the military six years ago. I wouldn't give them any names, though they already had Afia and Jack's names. I lied and said that Afia and I never slept together, that we were just friends, and she was my beard, protecting my secret. They didn't need to know any more than that. They asked about any relationships I had while in the military, and thankfully, Kelly told me not to answer that. *It's none of their fucking business anyway.*

They wanted to know about my relationship with Jamel, from the beginning. I told them all of it: meeting him at the pharmacy, the two dates before I ghosted him, and how later, we rekindled the relationship. We've been together since October 17, 2009. I left out the steamier parts of our relationship but did tell them about the first time we were intimate. I admitted that I lied to everyone for years about my relationship with Jamel until I decided to slowly come out of the closet. Last year, I told all of my friends, and this past winter, I told my youngest sister, Angie.

I told them about how I came out to my parents, drunk and sloppy at Angie's birthday dinner last month. It was the best decision I had ever made. I told them about the fight between Jack and my brother that same night because of the racist and homophobic epithets he yelled at Jamel and me. I told them of the conversation I had with my mother a week later that solidified my relationship with her, and how, for the first time, she acknowledged my father's abuse. My mother and sisters did not disown me because of my sexuality but instead embraced me and embraced Jamel as the man in my life. And that was probably what really set Owen off, the fact that I was being accepted as a gay man by my family.

Gram and Merchant had me there for hours. Kelly made them take a break to get me something to drink, and I chose water instead of coffee. I wish they would have offered me tequila. We went over what happened at the house again, and I stuck to my story because it was the truth.

"But why did you go for the gun?" Merchant asked me for the third time. "Why not join the fight, use your fists to fight back? Together, the two of you younger men could have taken the old man. Why did you go for the gun?"

"I told you: he was going to kill Jamel. He was most likely going to kill me too."

"But did he say that? Did he at any point say, 'I'm going to kill you' or 'I'm going to kill your partner'?"

"He didn't have to. I know my father. You have no idea how dangerous that man is."

"But Owen didn't come to the house with a weapon, Connor. You said yourself that Owen has a collection of guns, from .38's to AK-47's. If he wanted to kill you or Jamel, wouldn't he have just grabbed one of his guns before he made the trip to your house? Don't you think that's what your father would have done?"

"Don't answer that," Kelly said. "It's not his job to determine why his father did or did not bring a weapon to the home."

Merchant breathed out in frustration. "Here's my problem with all this, Connor. It's not that I don't believe you. I believe you. I believe that every single abusive thing that you say happened, happened. I met the old man, and he's not a very nice person. He's a cold sonofabitch. He kind of reminds me of my own old man, who was a functioning alcoholic by day and an asshole by night. So, I believe you."

He leaned in again, pressing his fingertips on the table. "But here's where I'm struggling. I think if Owen wanted to kill you, he would have. He sounds like a very calculating man. He would have just shown up and the moment you opened the door, blasted you and Jamel right through it. And then it would have been him sitting here instead of you. But he didn't do that. Yeah, he probably wanted to scare you, threaten you, but not actually kill you.

"But you? *You* grabbed the gun. Instead of fighting him off your partner, you went across the living room, into the dining room, opened the safe. The safe has a code I'm assuming, correct?"

I hesitated, but then answered, "Yes."

"Right!" said Merchant, almost excitedly. "You were conscious enough to put in the code. Once? Twice?"

Fuck. I knew where he was taking this, but I answered him anyway. "Once."

"*Riiiiight.* You only had to put it in once because you were perfectly aware of what you were doing. You went across two rooms, put in the security code, grabbed the loaded weapon—By your own account, you went for Jamel's Sig because his was loaded but your Magnum was not. You went for the loaded weapon and fired across two rooms. Maybe you were aiming for his head and only hit his shoulder."

"It sounds like you're making closing arguments, counselor," Kelly droned. He almost sounded bored. "Get to it so we can get out of here."

Merchant glared at my attorney, then rose. "Connor's not going anywhere except to arraignment."

"You gotta be fucking kidding me!" Kelly also got up. "On what evidence?"

"I just told you, Lirion. Get your client ready for trial."

"Bullshit charges! I'll get them thrown out during the arraignment. You just watch me."

But Merchant was already putting back on his suit jacket. Then he leaned over the desk and got in my face, almost nose to nose. "I know you tried to kill your father, Corporal. I know you wanted to kill your father last night, and Jamel probably stopped you from doing so. He's going to cover for you, but it won't be enough to save you. I'm going to nail your ass to the wall, and not in the way you'd like."

"That's enough!" Major Wendell stood too, his voice rumbling like thunder.

Merchant didn't budge. He stared me down, and I stared right back, anger burning in my chest. I was careful to keep my breathing even. He squinted, the top of his lip curling upward. My jaw twitched. "You want to murder me right now, don't you?" he asked quietly.

Not murder. Maybe beat the shit out of this cocky bastard, but not murder.

Kelly bent over, his hot breath between our faces. "Alex, you have three seconds to back up, or I'm getting the Rhode Island Bar on the phone and telling them that you are actively trying to intimidate my client. Back. The. Fuck. Up. *Now.*"

Merchant blew air out through his nose, but straightened. He grabbed his notepad off the desk. "Back to the hole he goes," he told Gram. As he walked out of the interrogation room, he added, "Connor will be charged with second degree attempted murder. Arraignment is tomorrow. Sleep tight, Corporal."

"Shit," Kelly muttered.

Gram shook his head. "It fits, Counselor, I'm sorry. It may not have been planned or premeditated, but he sure did try to make it happen without due cause." He grabbed the wrapped Sig and followed the ADA.

Kelly sighed. "Okay, we'll get these charges thrown out at court tomorrow and get a much lesser charge in. Then we'll take an even lesser plea. In the meantime, talk to no one, and I mean no one. It's not uncommon for them to throw someone in the cell with you to try to get you to admit to something. No talking."

I nodded. "Yes, sir," I said, sounding a hell of a lot more confident than I really was.

"Don't worry, Connor. I promise you: you're going home tomorrow."

"Okay, sir." I felt defeated.

"Stop calling me 'sir.' I said I'm a *retired* Army Specialist." He smiled at me.

I chuckled a little, despite the dread slowly filling my chest. "Okay, si— okay, Mr. Kelly."

"Lirion is fine. Or Kelly," he said. He turned to the Major. "I'm going to prepare this case with my firm. I'll come by the house later, and we can talk to Jamel together."

"I'll be at their house in West Warwick. Come by there instead," the Major told him.

"Okay, will do." Kelly shook my hand. "You're coming home tomorrow."

"Okay s—Okay Mr. Kel—*ah*... Lirion."

He laughed. "Keep working on it." He gathered his papers and put them in his briefcase.

I stood up and stretched, my body aching from sitting in that fold up chair for the last three hours. The Major touched my shoulder. "Hang in there, son. You're going to be just fine."

Jamel's dad started calling me son two weeks ago. At our first annual 4th of July barbecue, he pulled me aside and told me that if I ever needed a father figure then to look to him, that he'd be there for me. Who knew we'd be put to the test so quickly? But so far, he was showing up more than my father ever could or would. I don't know how he was able to sit in this room with me, but I am so grateful he was.

I decided to tease him, something I would have never done before with the serious and austere Army Major Wendell Jones. "Thanks, Dad. Can we go fishing when I get out of here?"

His old face crinkled up into a smile. "Funny. Now I see why Jamel likes you much."

I chuckled. He squeezed my shoulder. Before he could pull away, I gave him a hug. He awkwardly hugged me back, patting my back a few times before dropping his hands, not used to being affectionate. I almost chuckled again. The man wasn't warm and fuzzy, but fuck, I wished he really was my dad. He squeezed my shoulder one more time and left the room with my attorney.

A moment later, the same officer came in. He avoided direct eye contact. "Hold your wrists out."

I stepped closer to him and did so. Once he put the cuffs on me, I stepped even closer so that we were nose-to-nose, although he was slightly shorter than me. He drew in a short breath and his eyes widened.

"What are you doing?" he asked quietly.

"Nothing," I said back just as quietly, holding eye contact with him. "Lead the way, officer." *Sure, I'm facing murder charges and probably going to prison for the next 20 years, but why not flirt with the closeted cop? See? I do crazy shit.*

He led me by my arm out into the hall. Merchant was still there, talking with one of the other detectives, probably about some other poor bastard he was trying to rollover. He smiled at me as I passed, raising his coffee cup. I hated that cocky bastard. He reminded me of an older version of my brother.

When we got through the double doors, I turned my attention back to the guy holding my arm. "What's your name?"

"*Officer* Pike," he said without looking at me.

I nodded. "Nice to meet you, Officer Pike. And thank you for not treating me like a criminal."

"You *are* a criminal," he retorted.

"Innocent until proven guilty," I reminded him.

His scoff came out sounding more like a snort, making me giggle. Then he giggled. He walked me toward the cell I just came from. It had somehow gotten more crowded in the last few hours.

I sighed. "Do I really have to go in there, Officer Pike?" I stared, unblinking. I knew my eyes were mesmerizing him.

Speechless, he stared at me, then swallowed hard. "C'mon."

He led me to a smaller cell at the end of the hall, using his key to open the gate. It was much quieter down there. "Since you're going to be here for the next 24 hours, I figured you should at least have a bench to sleep on."

I stepped in, and he closed the bars behind me. I held out my wrists through the slot and he took the cuffs off. I massaged my wrists. "Thank you, Officer Pike."

The cop looked at a loss for words again. "You're welcome," he managed. "Good luck with … everything."

I shrugged. "Well, that homophobic asshole Merchant already said he's going to try to nail my ass to the wall, and not in the way I like, so it's safe to assume I'm going to need all the luck I can get."

"It's not because you're gay!" he blurted out. His face immediately flushed.

I sidled closer to the bars. "What do you mean?"

He came closer too and spoke in a low tone. "ADA Merchant. It's not because you're gay. He's coming after you because you're … pretty." I could see the color rising in his cheeks, but he didn't turn away this time. "I think he was like a nerd in high school and college and grew into his looks. He doesn't like pretty boys, the ones that get all the girls. And boys. The ones that seem to have all the luck. The ones that always get over because, you know… they're…"

"Hot?" I smiled.

He smiled back. "Yeah. Hot."

I nodded. "I'll try to make myself less appealing then."

He snickered. "That's not possible." He blanched. "Fuck. Um…" He stepped back and turned around. "I gotta go. I can't… I have a boy—I'm just going to go."

He rushed away. "He's a lucky man," I called out loud enough for him to hear but not loud enough for my voice to carry.

He turned and smiled widely at me. "Not as lucky as your boyfriend." Then, he added very quietly, "If it was me, I'd grab the gun too."

I liked Officer Pike. But I also remembered what Kelly had said about being careful who I spoke to, so I didn't acknowledge what he said. "Thanks again for the quiet cell."

"You're welcome." He stared into my eyes for another few seconds, probably contemplating all that could have been back there in the cell. But then, he turned around and walked back down the hall.

I laid down on the bench and put one knee up, my arm over my eyes. *I know they said only the guilty sleep but fuck it. I'm exhausted.* I closed my eyes and relived the last time Jamel and I made love, yesterday morning before we went to work, and fell asleep dreaming about the taste of his cum in the back of my throat.

♥

I sat on the side of the courtroom the next morning, with a few other handcuffed individuals waiting to be called up. Kelly sat in the rear with The Major, Jamel, and surprisingly, my little sister Angie. When Jamel came in, my heart started pumping faster as it always did. We didn't smile at each other; he just did a little nod and I did the same. I didn't look at him again.

The judge was an older man with a round face and graying hair who looked a bit like my father. His last name was O'Cannan, so it was probably the Irish roots we shared. I watched Merchant work. He was a good prosecutor, I had to admit. Almost all of his charges went through because he laid out evidence in a thoughtful and legal way. As quickly as people were led to the tables to make their plea, was as quickly as they were shuttled out in cuffs. Nobody went back out through the double doors to freedom. I was not hopeful at all.

After about an hour and a half, my name was called. I stood up and so did Kelly. We met at the table. "You plead not guilty, then you don't say another word," he said quietly.

"Yes, sir," I whispered.

The bailiff called out, "The People of The State of Rhode Island and Providence Plantations vs Corporal Connor Adrian McIntyre."

"Proceed," O'Cannan said.

Merchant began, "Your Honor, the People are charging Corporal Connor Adrian McIntyre with Second Degree Attempted Murder."

"How does the client plead?" the judge asked.

"Not guilty, Your Honor, sir," I said calmly.

"What's the grounds?" the judge asked Merchant.

He started with, "Your Honor, by his own admission Connor shot his father, Staff Sergeant Owen Matthew McIntyre with a SIG Sauer P226 pistol with the 9×19mm chamber legally registered to his domestic partner and homeowner Sergeant Jamel Josiah Jones. We believe he intended to end the senior McIntyre's life."

Kelly spoke up. "Your Honor, we refute that claim wholeheartedly. Staff Sergeant Owen Matthew McIntyre barged into their home and attacked both Connor and his partner, Jamel. Any actions after the initial aggression by the senior Mr. McIntyre would fall under self-defense of home and property. We ask that these charges be dismissed with prejudice."

"Your Honor," Merchant said, "Connor has a long and tumultuous history with his father. By his own account, his father was abusive, homophobic, and racist. We do not believe that Connor premeditated to bring about the death of his own father. However, we do believe that he intended to cause severe bodily harm—"

Kelly cut him off, "And again, Your Honor, once the senior McIntyre forced his way into the home—"

"Forced?" Merchant looked at Kelly, surprised. "I believe Connor opened the door and let him in, did he not?"

"And the first thing Owen did was choke him by his shirt collar and push him over the threshold. That would constitute as barging in, would it not?"

"Not nec—"

"Hey!" the judge yelled. "Knock it off, fellas. This is an arraignment, not a trial." They both quieted. "ADA Merchant, is there any evidence to suggest that this wasn't self-defense? Are there lesser charges considered?"

"As of right now, no, Your Honor. The perpetrator has only to cause serious bodily harm and to know that the act could result in death. Connor made the conscious decision to grab a dangerous weapon instead of intervening in the fight. Once he made the decision to grab the gun, it went from self-defense to second degree attempted murder."

"The boy was scared of his father, Your Honor. He was afraid of what his father might do to him and the love of his life. He reacted on impulse out of fear," said Kelly.

"The *boy* is a 28-year-old decorated Marine and Iraq war veteran. He reacted on impulse, but not out of fear. It was out of passion and hatred for his father."

"You have no evidence of that!" Kelly yelled.

"He hasn't lived with his father in two years. He wasn't afraid of his father anymore, Counselor," Merchant said.

"After living for over 20 years with this type of physical and psychological abuse, one does not simply stop being afraid, Counselor," Kelly retorted.

"Hey!" The judge banged his gavel this time. Both lawyers got quiet again. He looked at me and then looked away, saying more to himself, "Jesus, this is going to be a shitshow, isn't it?" No one refuted that assessment as he rubbed his forehead. "Alex, add a lesser charge or this ends today."

Merchant looked around thoughtfully, but something told me he expected this. "Attempted voluntary manslaughter."

Kelly threw his hands up in frustration. "How is that better!?"

"I'm sorry, Kelly," the judge said, "but this is going forward. The charges of Second Degree Attempted Murder and Attempted Voluntary Manslaughter stand. Bail?"

"The People ask for ten million dollars in bail," the ADA said confidently.

Holy. Shit. My mouth dropped open. "*What?*"

"Are you crazy!?" Kelly yelled.

The judge murmured, "God damnit, Alex."

"This is a serious charge, and it needs to be taken seriously," Merchant said.

"There is no way he can afford that, and you know it, Alexander," Kelly snarled.

"Good! Because there's nothing to stop him from going after his father again. This is the only way we can keep the senior McIntyre safe."

"Except he didn't go after his father the first time, his father came to *his* house to cause bodily harm to him!" Kelly raised his voice.

"Lower it, ADA Merchant," the judge said tiredly.

"No!" Merchant said, almost nastily. "Connor McIntyre needs to stay in jail and consider the damage that he's done to his family."

"Your Honor, please," Kelly pleaded. "Like ADA Merchant just said, he's a decorated Marine and Iraq war veteran. He's never been in any trouble with the law. He runs an organization that helps other vets. He's not a danger to others, including his father. He'll surrender his passport. Make it reasonable so that Connor can return to his home to prepare for the fight of his life."

But the judge seemed to hardly hear my attorney. He narrowed his eyes at the prosecutor. "Lower it, significantly," he said again. "Or I will."

But the ADA must have been feeling himself with all the wins he had that morning. "No," he said unequivocally. "Ten million dollar bail. That's the People's stance."

O'Cannan was not happy being challenged. He finally turned his attention to me. "Corporal Connor

McIntyre, will you surrender your passport and stay 500 feet away from your father's home, person, and place of business?"

"Yes, sir," I said automatically. "I work in Rockville, but the apartment complex I manage is a good three miles away from my family's house. As long as I go the long way around town, it should be fine."

"Don't let him out, Your Honor," Merchant said and not in a nice tone.

"I think you've forgotten who runs the courtroom, Alex," the judge said. He turned back to me. "The defendant is released ROR. Stay away order is issued for Staff Sergeant Owen McIntyre. The defendant must stay 500 feet from his person, home, and business at all times until this matter is concluded in a U.S. court."

"What the f—" Merchant had to catch himself. He was steaming mad but the judge continued, ignoring him completely and speaking directly to me.

"No contact at all, including telephone, mail, email, or any other technological means of communication. The defendant will surrender his passport to the courts. You will not leave the state, not even to Connecticut or Massachusetts. You will not engage in any illegal activity while this order stands. Violate any part of this order and the ten million dollar bail will be invoked. Do you understand me, Corporal McIntyre?"

I responded, "Yes, sir, Your Honor, sir."

"This is a travesty!" Merchant yelled angrily.

The judge sat up straighter. "Say 'travesty' again, and you'll be saying it from a cell in contempt." The ADA glared at him. After a moment, he banged his gavel. "You're free to go, Corporal."

Merchant slammed his papers on the tabletop as the guard came over and took off my cuffs. "Go home. I'll come by later for you to sign some papers," Kelly said, touching my shoulder.

I ran, practically jumping over the short wall that separated the proceedings from the spectators. Jamel was already in the aisle with his arms open. I flew into them, throwing my arms around his neck. He returned the favor, wrapping his arms around me and squeezing me. We stood there for a moment as I closed my eyes and breathed in his scent. The scent of home. I could feel how fast his heart was beating against my chest.

He ran his hands through my hair, making me raise my head from his shoulder. Before I had a chance to think, he rubbed his nose against mine and softly kissed my lips. I knew the whole courtroom was watching, and for once, I didn't care. He pulled back slightly and looked me in my eyes. As always, I found myself swimming in his silver irises.

His eyes left me momentarily to look around as if asking, *Is this okay?*

He knew PDA made me nervous. I hadn't been out long enough for these things not to matter to me. I didn't know if I would ever be okay with it. But at that moment, I needed him. So, I answered him by pressing two soft, gentle kisses on his full lips. He rubbed his nose against mine again and took my hand, lacing our fingers. I didn't look around to see who saw us. I kept my eyes and my heart focused on him. Together, we left the courthouse and went home.

♥

We drove to the house in silence with his arm around me, my head against his shoulder and my hand on his knee. When we got to our block, I noticed the cars right away.

"Fuck, Mel," I said quietly.

He pulled into the driveway behind my Infiniti Q50. "They all love you and wanted to be here for you when you got home."

I frowned and said, "Or they wanted to be here for you in case I didn't come home."

I looked up at him. He cupped my chin to press his lips against mine. "They won't stay long, promise."

I nodded and we left his truck together. Although I knew they were all there, seeing everyone that I love crowded in the living room with worried faces overwhelmed me. The dogs, Mage and Diesel, broke the silence by barking loudly and jumping all over me. But of course, Lovie got to me first.

Afia threw her arms around me and started crying. My eyes welled up with tears as I held her, careful not to squish her swollen belly, but I sniffed them back. She held me for a long time, and everyone let her. They all knew she was the second most important thing to me besides Jamel. Mary Kate, my little sister, hugged me right behind her, also crying. It reminded me that I forgot to hug my baby sister at the courthouse; I only had eyes for Mel. Mina hugged me next, nice and tight, her face damp with tears. Winter, next in line, wasn't crying but I didn't expect her to; her beautiful heart-shaped face was stone, and her hazel eyes were like glass. She was more angry than sad for me, and I appreciated the shit out of her for that. Henrietta, Mina's sister, hugged me too, another nice, tight embrace.

I looked around for my mother, and she was not there, but Jamel's mother, Mama Denita, was. She was the last of the women in the room to hug me. She pulled my neck down to her 5'4" height and said, "I'm so glad you're home. I love you, Connor."

"I love you too, Mama Denita."

She touched my face. "It's gonna be okay, baby." I nodded and she stepped back.

One by one, Jamel's brothers came to hug me. Tyrell, Afia's husband, hugged me first, which was surprising since last month he tried to take my head off in this same room. We were not exactly friends. Then Donell and Lavell. My friends, Liam, Sam, Brayden, and BJ, hugged me too.

"It was bound to happen one day," BJ remarked. I just patted his arm in response. If there was one other person in the room besides Afia that knew of Owen's abuse when we were growing up, it was BJ. Afia kept my secrets while BJ kept Matty's.

The door opened and Angie and The Major came in. She ran up to me and hugged me. "I'm sorry I didn't—" I began.

"It's okay. Don't apologize," she said into my chest. "You needed Jamel. Now I need you." I stroked her blonde locks. Mary Kate came back over, and I held them both, grateful for my sisters' support and love.

"Where's Mom?" I asked.

They looked at each other. "She's … not allowed … to see you," Mary Kate admitted. Of course Owen would keep my mother from me. *Fuck him for that.*

"She'll find a way, Connor," Mama Denita spoke up. "Katie loves you and will find a way." I nodded at my pretty-much mother-in-law. Jamel's mother and my mother were close so I knew they would talk.

Ethan wrapped me up in a brotherly hug. I didn't know why it made me want to tear up, but I had to sniff the emotion back again. I liked Ethan. He was married to my best friend, close friends with my boyfriend, and gave me a job at The Residence, but he and I weren't friends in our own right. It wasn't like we hung out without Jamel or Jack present. But he still held me in a loving embrace and rubbed my back. He was a gentle soul, and I could see how Jack fell in love with him so easily. Eventually, he let me go.

Jack was last. He held my face in both of his hands, his thumbs rubbing my cheeks. His green eyes shone brightly and they were sad. His noticeable dimples were turned in as his face was set in a frown. As we stared at each other, all I could think about was how I should have told Jack about my father's abuse when we were younger. He would have supported me; hell, he would have helped me escape. Maybe our lives would have been completely different.

He must have been thinking the same because tears started falling out of his eyes in a steady stream. That alone made my emotions boil over. My face contorted and my shoulders shook. I started sobbing, and he pulled me into a tight hug. His hug was completely different than the hug his husband just gave me, but just as effective. We held each other and cried on each other's shoulders.

After a while, Ethan came over and rubbed my back, then I felt other hands touch and rub me comfortingly. I feared how everything would turn out, but at that moment, I was so happy. I felt seen, protected, and loved by every single person in the room. Maybe I was a lucky man too.

CHAPTER 3

THAT'S NOT DONNY.

~~~September 2012~~~

Jamel and I took the drive over to North Providence, the Allendale section. Instead of driving to his family home, we went a few blocks over to Tyrell and Afia's tiny rental house. They just got married in May and already had a little one, Tykeya Adina Jones. We saw them last week in the hospital when she gave birth, but we wanted to wait until she was home to drop off more equipment. Lovie—my nickname for my best friend because she's the most lovable person on the planet—had all these superstitions about not calling the baby's name out loud before she was born and not setting up the nursery, so we came over to help Ty. He was struggling to put everything together at the last minute.

We unloaded the things out of Jamel's cherry red Ford F150 pickup: a Pack & Play, lots of clothes, a
~~~

couple of blankets my mother had knitted, and a shit ton of nursing stuff because Lovie was determined to nurse her for the foreseeable future. Even though Jamel had a key, he rang the doorbell.

Donny opened the door looking high as fuck. "Heeeeey," he drew out the greeting, smiling with his bloodshot eyes.

I laughed and Jamel shook his head at his little brother. He filled his arms with baby things. "Go make yourself useful," he told him. Donny laughed but took the bulky Pack & Play and a bag of nursing pads inside.

Afia was sitting in a rocking chair with a wrapped bundle in her arms. She looked perfect, her almond skin glowing, her shoulder length hair pulled back into a ponytail. She looked up and smiled at me, slowly rocking back and forth.

Ty came out from the back of the one-story home. "Hey, Mel. Hey, Connor. Thanks for coming."

He led the way to the second bedroom of the house. It had been painted, at least, a nice lavender color with white bunnies on the wall. Other than that, it might as well have been a storage room. Boxes were everywhere, baby clothes spilled out of bags, and worst of all, the crib was in pieces on the floor.

"Shit." I said what everyone was thinking.

Ty looked at me sadly. "I know. I've been trying to organize all this but ... this is crazy." He put his knuckles on his hips and pouted. "Help?"

Donny and I laughed. Jamel, taking charge, started giving out orders. "Connor, take the bags of clothes into the living room and separate them by age range and season. Donny, grab all the nursing items and take them into the main bedroom to categorize them. Anything associated with feeding bottles, like the nipples and the cleaning products go together; pumping equipment like the pumping bottles, freezer bags, and Mother's Milk tea bags and other lactation supplements go together; nursing bras, tees, and Lanolin go together. Ty, we're moving the rest of these boxes into the hallway and grabbing the instructions, so we can put the crib together. Got it?"

"Sir, yes sir," we all chorused, teasing him.

He waved his hand dismissively. "Yeah, yeah, yeah, get to work."

We laughed but did as we were told. I knew why he put me on clothing duty in the living room. Hanging with Lovie and the baby was the real reason why I was there, not to do manual labor.

I started pulling the bags one by one into the living room. Afia watched me as she held the sleeping baby. Once I was done with five bags of new clothes and three more bags of hand-me-downs from her sister's first pregnancy, I sat on the floor in front of her and started going through them.

"You look good," I told her as I put all the plain, white onesies in a pile.

She scoffed. "I look tired. I am nursing and pumping every three hours around the clock."

"Pumping and nursing? Why both?"

"Because I need to nurse her from each breast, and then empty them out by pumping to build up my supply. My milk just came in a few days ago so I want to keep it going. If I don't pump after nursing, I'll get engorged, and that shit is painful."

"Engorged?" I snorted and she shook her head.

"What are you, 12?" she playfully scolded, making me giggle. "Put that red onesie to the side, it has bottoms to it somewhere in one of the other bags." I did as she asked, and she continued to direct my sorting. "Anyway, I'm following my lactation consultant to ensure I can nurse for the next two years."

"Two years? Won't that baby have like … teeth?"

"Yes, she will be walking and talking and still come to me for mama's milk," she said proudly.

"Then your tits will really be engorged." I laughed.

She laughed with me. "Yeah, well they already grew like half a cup size, and that makes me happy."

We giggled again. Afia had always been sensitive about her barely B cups. "Where is your mom?" I asked. "I expected Dr.. Adina to be ruling the house right now."

"Mommy and Mama Denita are out having lunch. They're taking turns driving me crazy." She rolled her eyes. "'Don't cover her up too much, it's too hot. Put socks on her feet, it's too cold.' Blah blah blah."

"Oh, you knew exactly what it was going to be like having the two of them here," I chided her.

"I know," she whined. "I'm about to put them on a schedule so they aren't here on the same day." She pressed her lips together, watching me sort. "Your mom came to see me."

I looked at her, surprised. "Yeah? When?"

"Two days ago, with Angie. It was a nice surprise. She said that you were bringing me the blankets she knitted, but she wanted to bring something just for me, and gave me a basket of handmade soaps with essential oils in them. Lavender for sleep, orange for alertness, peppermint for stress relief. Some other ones she labeled."

I smirked. "She's still hurt that you weren't really my girlfriend all that time. I think she would have really liked having you as a daughter-in-law."

"Yeah well, maybe she shouldn't have given birth to a gay son," Afia teased, making me chuckle. "She looked… I don't know… tired, I guess. Sad."

"Any bruises?" I asked without meeting her eyes.

"No," she said quietly. "Not that I could see. Maybe he's not taking it out on her."

"He is," I said definitively.

My mom and I used to meet on Thursday mornings for breakfast right before my day started at The Starling Residence where I was a property manager. Owen put a stop to that when he found out I was released, so I hadn't seen my mother since the week before my birthday. When I called her, she wouldn't answer but would send me a random text later to say something like, "Hi Connor. Make sure you're eating your vegetables. I love you." It was kind and frustrating at the same time. My mother can be incredibly sweet and incredibly fake. You have to be when you have an abusive husband.

"Something's wrong," Afia said, interrupting my thoughts.

She jerked her chin toward the hallway. Donny was walking toward the front door with a rolled up blunt behind his ear. He must have sensed us watching him because he turned and gave us a smile. "I'll be right out front, y'all."

He stepped out and Lovie shook her head. "Tyrell is going to kick him out."

"And rightfully so," I stated. "He can't come in here reeking of marijuana when you have a newborn."

"But something is wrong, Connor. He used to get high once in a while, but not this continuous Cheech and Chong shit. *Stuff.* I gotta stop cursing."

I smiled at her. "I don't think Tykeya understands just yet."

"Doesn't matter. I need to practice using other words. I'm a mother now," she said proudly.

I giggled. "Okay, Lovie." It was all she ever dreamed of: being a wife and a mother.

I went back to sorting clothes. "Connor, go talk to him," Afia urged. "Find out what's going on. He's been smoking weed all week, nonstop. Wake and bake. Tweak and sleep. That's not Donny."

"Is there a reason you are asking me instead of Ty or even Mel?"

"Because Ty has a lot going on, obviously. I would ask Mel, but I think Donny will be more open with you. Please, Connor?" she pleaded.

I put down the pink leggings that I was holding. "Okay, I'll talk to him."

I made my way outside and found Donny smoking a few feet from the front door. He didn't look at me as I approached but passed the blunt to me. I thought briefly about the judge threatening to have my balls in a ten million dollar vice if I did anything illegal, but I pulled from the blunt anyway. I held my breath for five seconds, then slowly let it out. I immediately felt relaxed. I hadn't smoked cigarettes in years and smoking pot wasn't really my thing, but I smoked with Donny from time to time. I handed the blunt back to him.

Donny took a long pull, held it longer than I did, then let it out through his nose. Donell's skin complexion was closer to Jamel's, darker than Tyrell but not as dark as my lover. They shared similar features: strong jawline, almond-shaped eyes, full lips and small ears. But Donny's eyes were brown, like their father and younger brother, Lavell, who was away at MIT. Only Ty and Mel had the gray eyes of their mother.

Like Lavell, Donny let his wavy hair grow out. Lavell's hair was past his shoulders, but he permanently locked his twists at sixteen. Jamel kept a close crop at all times, preferring a Caesar cut. Ty's hair was short and curly on top of his head, the sides shaved down. But Donell's hair was inches past his shoulders, thick and wavy. He typically had it either in a ponytail or braided back, but it was hanging loose down his back that day.

Donell did seem to be heavily contemplating something. We passed the blunt back and forth a few times in silence. "What's wrong?" I finally asked.

He sighed deeply. "Connor, how did you go so long without telling anyone who you really were? Your sexuality? That's a huge secret to keep, especially from people you love."

I figured this was not really about me, so I gave him the abbreviated version. "It wasn't easy. There were plenty of times I just wanted to blurt it out. It had been eating me up inside since I was a teen. Besides being deathly afraid of my father, I think it was the fear of how people were going to react to the news that kept me from doing so. But when I finally did, the complete opposite happened. Everyone that I loved showed me that they loved me right back and accepted my truth. They forgave me for keeping them in the dark for so long, and they continued loving me." I turned to him. "Whatever it is, we can handle it."

"My father is going to kill me," Donny said seriously.

He must have done something super illegal. The THC was getting to me and I couldn't help but make a joke. "Are *yoooou* about to be sitting in prison for second degree murder? I'm sorry, *attempted.*"

He smirked. "No, not that bad."

I put my hand on his shoulder. "Then we can handle it. Whatever it is, Don, I'll stand by you."

He sighed deeply again. Then he dropped the half-smoked blunt in the grass and stepped on it. "Let's take a walk."

He put his hands in his pockets and started walking, so I followed him. I mirrored his posture, sliding my hands into my pockets too. We walked about a block down from the house before he started talking. "My mama, she made a comment at the hospital last week. 'I'm so excited to have my first grandchild.'" He sighed. "It's not her first grandchild."

Holy shit! I wanted to say it out loud. My eyes bugged out my head, but luckily, he wasn't looking at me. He was looking straight ahead.

"Vanessa," he said, answering my next question before I could ask it.

Vanessa was his on and off again girlfriend from college. She went to Spellman and he was at Morehouse.

They were also both in Greek life, with Donny in Phi Beta Sigma and Vanessa being in Zeta Phi Beta. We had only met her once, a few years back when Jamel and I first started dating and she came over to their house for a barbecue. He had kept his relationship with her almost secretive. Jamel said it was because they didn't have very much in common except being in Greek life and having sex, but Donny didn't know how to let things go that needed to be let go. It wasn't surprising at all that they were still sleeping together. He took trips back down south to do Greek things, so I was sure they saw each other all the time, despite him living in Rhode Island and her living in Virginia.

"Boy or girl?" I asked.

He smiled. "Boy. DJ. Donell Junior. She didn't give him my last name though. That's okay."

I nodded. "Soooooo... why haven't you told anyone?"

He shrugged. "You know how The Major is. He feels very strongly about his sons being an example to men, especially black men, everywhere. Having a child out of wedlock? He's going to flip the fuck out."

"And marriage is out of the question?" I asked. Donny looked at me sideways then looked ahead again. "I'm just saying. People get married all the time for lots of reasons. You love her, right?"

"I do. Even more now that she had my son. But not enough to marry her. I know that sounds awful. Like she was good enough to sleep with but not to keep. But neither of us were looking for a relationship. We were just ... being familiar with each other. She really loves me though, and she would have been down for it. But she deserves to be with someone who wants to be committed to her. That's not me."

I nodded. "I know how it feels when someone else's feelings for you are stronger than your feelings for them."

"Exactly. And it wouldn't be fair to her to just be together for the sake of DJ. She doesn't need to be trapped by me because we created a life. I explained that to her, and she was hurt but she agreed."

"How old is DJ?" I hoped this kid wasn't walking and talking because that would be another holy shit moment.

"Three months. Almost four months, on the 25th of this month."

"You went nine months knowing you got someone pregnant and then the last four months hiding a baby and a baby-mama?"

"Yep." He nodded slowly.

"Yeah, The Major is going to murder you." I started giggling. I couldn't help it. Maybe smoking with Donny wasn't the best decision before this very serious conversation.

He started laughing too. "He is."

Suddenly we were both laughing hysterically. We had to stop walking and catch our breaths with how funny it was, although it was anything but funny. When we were able to compose ourselves, he reached out and hugged me. I hugged him back.

It's funny that hugging another man in the street doesn't come with an ounce of anxiety for me, except when it's Jamel. I feel like the whole world can tell we're fucking when we hold each other. I started laughing again.

Donny started laughing too, probably because of a random thought that popped in his own head. He wasn't a mind reader. Or was he?

Yeah, I'm high as fuck.

We got ourselves together again. "Did you mean it when you said you'd stand by me?" Donny asked. "Because they are all going to hate me, and I need someone in my corner."

I touched his shoulder. "They aren't going to hate you. Jamel is not going to hate you. You know this. Tyrell is not going to hate you. Lavell respects you, and he's still going to look up to his big brother. Your father is going to be disappointed, but he loves you. Even if he's never said the words, you know he does. And Mama Denita? Well, she doesn't have it in her to be mad at you for long."

He smiled, though he looked scared. "How do I come out and tell them?"

"Well, don't get drunk off of tequila and blurt it out in a crowded restaurant because that doesn't work for everyone," I joked, making him laugh again. I put my arm around his shoulders, and we began walking back to the house. "Tell Jamel first. He's not going to yell at you, and he can ease your father into it. Start there."

He sighed. "Okay."

I patted his shoulder. "So tell me about him. Tell me about your son DJ."

Donny smiled again. Apparently, he was there when he was born. He told his parents he had a frat emergency and took off when Vanessa called and said she was in labor. He told me that as soon as DJ came out and they laid him on Vanessa's chest, he felt his heart explode. When he held him, he knew he would never be the same. Donny stayed with her for four weeks and then came back home like nothing happened but had been taking the long drive and occasional flight every other week to see and spend time with his son. Vanessa had no idea that his parents didn't know.

When we got back to the house, Afia took one look at me and scowled. Tykeya was awake and she was nursing her. I smiled widely at her then patted Donny's back. He patted me back and went to finish sorting nipple pads from panty liners. I went back to sorting clothes.

As soon as she heard the bedroom door close, Afia started scolding me. "Connor! Damnit, I told you to get him talking, not get yourself high."

I giggled. "I'm sorry, but it was the only way. And we did speak."

"Well, what's wrong with him?" she asked. I made a show of zipping my mouth shut, turning a key in a lock, then throwing it away.

"Ugh!" she scoffed. "Just tell me he's okay."

"He's okay. But he's hiding something from everyone, and it's eating him up inside. He'll come clean soon."

Her eyes went wide. "Is he gay!?"

I laughed. "No. And if he was, that's not really a big deal in this family, considering they already have one gay son."

She laughed too. "Okay well, how bad is it?"

I began to do the shutting my mouth routine all over again and she scoffed. "Ugh, *shut up.*"

I laughed again as she switched breasts. I got a glimpse of her swollen mounds with dark areolas and huge nipples. She was right; her breasts were definitely bigger. I got a strong urge to touch them. The female body doesn't stir my loins anymore, but Afia was different. She is and will always be the most beautiful girl in the world.

She caught me staring. "Don't start appreciating my tits now. You had your chance," she said smugly, making me fall over with laughter. After she was done nursing and had burped her daughter, she asked, "Wanna hold your niece?"

I stood. "Yes, but let me wash my hands and take this outer layer off, just in case it smells like smoke."

She smiled. "See, you would be a great dad."

"Not happening, Lovie," I called out as I took off my long-sleeved shirt and made my way to the kitchen.

When I came back, I sat on the couch instead of the floor. Afia gently put the eight-pound baby in my arms. I sat back and held her, watching her look around sleepily.

"Thank you because I have to pee. And take a shower. I'll be back in like … 15 minutes. Maybe 20. You got this, right?" Afia didn't wait for a response before she disappeared down the hall.

I looked down at Tykeya. She had Afia's face shape and features except for her ears and gray eyes. That came from the Jones side of the family. "Hey, Keya, it's your Uncle Connor," I murmured softly. "You have a lot of uncles, but I'm going to be the one that you can talk to about boys and help you with your hairstyles like I did for your mom when she was a kid. You'd like that, right?"

I didn't notice Jamel until he leaned over the back of the couch right beside my shoulder. I flinched in surprise, then smiled at him. "So is that why these clothes are half done?" he asked. "Because you've been playing Nanny out here this whole time?"

I chuckled. "No, I just got the baby from Lovie a few minutes ago. I went on a walk with your little brother."

He sniffed. "You smell like you did."

I felt bad. "Oh, well then take her, because I don't want—"

"Don't worry. It's really faint. I was just teasing you." Jamel ran his hands through my hair. My throat rumbled and I closed my eyes. It felt amazing.

"Babies look good on you," I heard him say.

My eyes flew open. "I'm not having kids, Mel." I had already solidified that in my mind a long time ago and Jamel agreed to it.

He hesitated then continued to stroke my hair. "I know, Connor. We're not having kids. And I'm okay with that." He kissed the side of my head and smartly changed the subject. "Speaking of Donny, he asked us to give him a ride home. Said he needed to talk about something important. Did he tell you on your walk?"

"Yes. And he needs to tell you himself. Don't freak on him, okay? His biggest fear is that everyone will be mad and disappointed in him, and I know how that feels."

"Is my brother okay? Did he do something bad?" His hands stilled in my hair.

"Yes, he's fine. He didn't break the law. He just needs our support," I told him. "Now keep stroking my hair." He chuckled and ran his hand through my hair a few more times.

CHAPTER 4

BIG DADDY

After a few hours, we had the nursery set up with the clothes in the dresser and closet. We moved her rocking chair into the room so she could be close to the baby while she pumped. Finally, we placed my mother's blankets all over the house so that she would be comfortable in any room. Afia and Tyrell's mothers came back from their outing and started nagging her with motherly advice, so we took that as an opportunity to make our exit.

Donny jumped in the truck with us, and we drove southwest toward the family home where he lived. Donell took over Mel's old apartment on the bottom floor when we bought our house last year. Considering that Lavell lived in an apartment off campus in Cambridge with Chad, his college roommate from MIT, and would probably stay there when he graduated next year, Donny was the last member of his family to leave the nest.

Donny was quiet on the car ride over, and Jamel wasn't going to ask. But when we got to the house, he didn't open the car door. He just sat there looking sad. I was sitting in the middle, so I looked over at Mel and nodded at him. Then I tapped Donny's leg.

"Let me out. I'm going to go say hello to The Major. You, stay."

Donny reluctantly opened the door and stepped out. I patted his back as I passed him and closed the car door when he got back in. I went inside the quiet house, thinking about the times I would come over for dinner and it would be full and lively. So much had changed over the last couple of years, but all for the better. I grew up and matured being with Jamel, and his family was a huge part of my growth.

I found the old man in the kitchen trying to make dinner for himself. With Mama Denita practically living over at her new granddaughter's house, Major Wendel Jones had been left to his own devices. I watched him from the doorway as he burned his hand on a pot handle. "Shit," he hissed.

"Need some help?" I asked, amused.

He looked up. "Hey, Connor. What are you doing here?"

"We're dropping Donny off. Just wanted to come up and say hello, sir. But now I'm glad I did."

He gave me a wry look. "I've never been good at cooking. I could barely boil water when I met Denita. One of the first things she did was make me a home-cooked meal. And I never looked back."

I rolled up my sleeves and I looked into the frying pan. It looked like he was trying to make a pasta dish, but the fire was too high and the noodles were burning at the bottom. I pulled it off the stove.

"Here, let's get a new pan and start with the olive oil. The key is to sauté it first, then add in the boiled noodles."

Together, we cooked a simple pasta dish with little pieces of white meat chicken and bigger pieces of red, green and yellow peppers. We didn't talk much as we cooked, but we worked together as a team. "I could barely boil water when Mel came into my life too," I admitted. "We would cook together a lot in the beginning of our relationship so all of this I learned from him. Especially making pasta dishes, his favorite food."

"You're good at this," The Major told me.

"Cooking?"

"Leading," he said. "You're a natural born leader, like Jamel. That was probably my only concern about the nature of your relationship with my son: How two alpha males were going to fit together, compromise, and make it work."

I smiled. "Thank you, sir. That means a lot coming from you, another natural born leader." I was quiet for a moment, thinking about what he said. "I think I've been the one to step back and let him take the lead most of the time. I was able to let my guard down with him pretty early on because Jamel has always made me feel safe and comfortable to do so. Plus, he's a little older, wiser, and I trust him."

The Major looked into my eyes. "That, and I also think you've lived most of your life letting people take power from you. I understand you doing that with Jamel, your partner. Jamel will never take advantage of your trust in him. But you don't need to do that anymore, Connor. You're a man now. It's time you step into your power and position. Believe in yourself. Know what you're capable of, leading others just like you did when you were in Iraq. Trust your instincts and make smart decisions, regardless of how anyone else feels about it. You're still a corporal. Act like it."

I was a little speechless. I never saw myself as giving away my power but after he said it, I thought he might have been a little right. I allowed my father to have power over me for way too long. That's why I stayed at home, despite how toxic it was, until Jamel gave me a reason to leave. My desire to be with him was powerful enough to pull me away from my father's grasp. I may have unknowingly transferred some of that power and hold my father had on me onto Jamel.

I'd been afraid to step out and do things my own way for so long. But in order to really step out and do what I wanted to do, it would mean leaving Jamel behind in some ways. I had a lot of ideas of how I wanted Vinnie's Vet Buddies to expand that would require traveling to different parts of the country, connecting with national audiences and organizations. But I had attached myself to my boyfriend; I didn't know if I was ready to leave the nest that I had created for myself.

Thinking of leaving the nest had me thinking of Donny again. "Thank you, sir. And you're right, there are things that I want to do, but I'm afraid people won't accept the path that I want to create for myself. I don't want to disappoint people that I care about, like you."

He touched my shoulder. "As long as whatever decision you make, good or bad, you own up to it and stand by it like a man, you'll have my support. I don't agree with how you handled your father when he came to the house. But I understand it and I stand by it. And I'll support you through all of this."

I nodded. "Just like you would for any of your sons that make mistakes and own up to them, right, sir?" I looked him in the eyes, and he seemed to understand I was not just talking about me.

"Right." He nodded slowly. "Just like I would for any of my sons. Because you're one of them now."

"Thank you, sir." I nodded back.

He looked at me a moment longer. "Something I should know? About one of my sons?"

"Not anything that I could tell you, sir," I told him honestly.

He nodded again. He didn't say anything more and turned to grab a plastic bowl. "Here, you should take some of this food you made home with you." Before I could protest, he scooped the pasta into the bowl and put a cover on it.

I looked at the small bowl. "It's only enough for one."

"I know," he said with a wink.

That made me chuckle. I realized we had been there almost an hour, so I excused myself and went outside to see Jamel and Donny still in the truck. Donny looked miserable with his head down. Mel's face was unreadable. Donny nodded a few times as Mel spoke. Eventually, he opened the car door to leave, but Mel pulled him back and hugged him. Donny looked at me from over Jamel's shoulder, and I nodded at him.

Climbing out of the truck, Donny came over to give me a brief hug before heading inside. When I got into the passenger's side, Jamel didn't look at me. He quietly started the car and got on the road. I could tell he was taking in what Donny told him about his secret love child. I put my hand on his thigh as he drove us home.

When he pulled into the driveway, he turned the car off but didn't move. He sighed. "My father is going to flip the fuck out."

"Donny said the same thing. It's just kinda hard for me to imagine him flipping out, you know?"

"It doesn't happen often; my mama was usually the one to carry out the discipline while my father gave us his disappointed lectures. But you don't understand how my father feels about things like this. Black men feeding into racial stereotypes." He paused for a moment, then gave me an example.

"When Tyrell was seventeen, he got arrested for underaged drinking and driving under the influence. Ty and Donny were always getting into trouble and getting scolded by my dad for some typical adolescent things: drinking, smoking weed, throwing house parties when no one was home, stupid shit. But when he got arrested, that set my father over the edge. I was already in the Army when it happened, but apparently, The Major lost it. He hemmed Ty up by his shirt and slammed him against the wall, screaming that he disgraced himself and our family."

"Wow." I still couldn't see it. Major Jones hurting one of his sons the way my father hurt me? I couldn't fathom it.

"Yep. Donny and Lavell had to pull him off. Then he stopped talking to him. For two months. Not one word did he utter to his own son. Ty couldn't take the silent treatment anymore, so he came to see me on base and told me what happened. I got emergency family leave to bring him back. I had to sit them both down and mediate, first getting my father to hear him out. Then Ty begged for his forgiveness and promised never to drink and drive again, and while my father accepted it, their relationship wasn't solid at all.

"Ty had this air of always trying to please him, more so than the rest of us, but The Major always let him know he fell just short of his total approval. Ty has spent the last ten years making it up to him, leading a straight and narrow life. He rarely drinks and never gets drunk; he works hard right under my father's watchful eye. Even getting married, having kids. He loves Afia, don't get me wrong, but his desire to get married and raise a family at 27 had a lot to do with making his father proud of him. Which he is now, very."

"I would have never guessed their relationship was so bad."

"You never wondered why The Major waited until I came home to pass the construction business to me? Why he made me his foreman instead of Ty, even though he's been working with him since he was 16-years-old?" Mel asked.

"Honestly, I never thought about it. I assumed The Major wanted you to lead the business because you're the eldest. You're next in line to take over for him."

"But I was gone for seven years, Con. Ty knew the ins and outs of construction and maintenance repairs way more than I did. I had to play catch up when I got back. And even still, I wasn't sure if I wanted to lead the company. The truth is, I'm still not sure. But the family business is Ty's whole life."

"What do you think The Major is going to do?" I asked him. "Because Donell isn't sixteen and got someone pregnant. He's 25-years-old. You think The Major is going to slam him into a wall too?"

"I don't know, Con. But I know I need to be there, just in case he does go off."

I nodded. "So have it here." He looked at me. "Invite them both over so Donny can tell him in a neutral place and have our support."

He nodded thoughtfully. "That might work. And sooner rather than later."

"We'll set it up for next weekend." I enjoyed bringing people together at my house for dinner parties anyway.

But Jamel shook his head. "Next weekend we're supposed to see Lavell. Remember, he and Chad are throwing a party at the new apartment."

"Oh. Right." I sat back and tried not to be annoyed. I wouldn't be going because MIT was in another state, and I couldn't cross state lines. But everyone else was, including my sisters Angie and MK.

He gently stroked the side of my hair. "Sorry, baby. I told you I would stay home with you."

I shook my head. "Of course you won't. Go to your brother's housewarming. I'll be fine. I'll get takeout. Watch porn. Jack off a couple of times until I fall asleep. I'll be fine."

He smiled at me. "Let's go to bed."

God, yes. My high had worn off, but the lingering effect kept my dick semi-hard all day. I was ready to get fucked.

We went inside the house through the garage door and came up the stairs leading to the kitchen. Jamel poured a glass of Hennessy, his drink of choice when he was stressed out, and took a sip before he poured me a smaller glass. I took my swig in one gulp and put the empty glass on the counter. Without another word, I began to strip.

I took off my long-sleeved shirt and dropped it on the floor of the kitchen. Then I took off my t-shirt and added it to the pile. He watched me while taking another small sip. I walked backward, slipping out of my shoes first, then taking off my socks. He followed me slowly, watching me, still holding onto his glass and sipping little by little. I wasn't smiling and neither was he. I made it to the bottom of the stairs and paused, still in my jeans. He came close, and I could feel the heat radiating off his body. I went up one stair backward, so I was towering over him, then another.

He reached up with his free hand and touched the ridges of my abdominal muscles. He let his fingertips graze downward on one side and touched all four mounds like he was counting them in his head. He slid his fingers right below my belly button to the other side and counted four more going up. I let him explore my body the way he saw fit.

His traced the underline of my right pec and slid across to my left pec. His two fingers, middle and index, rose higher to rub my dark pink nipple. My breath hitched when he touched me; my nipples are extremely sensitive. Before he could do the same to my left one, I went backward up the next stair. Then the next one. He smirked at me, and I smiled slyly back. When I got to the sixth step, he finished his drink and carefully placed the empty glass on the bottom stair; then he started to slowly climb. I let him pursue me up the stairs, still walking backward to keep my eye on him. He watched me lustfully.

When I got to the top, I slowly walked backward toward our bedroom. When he got to the top landing, he moved quickly, startling me. Jamel pushed my body against the wall and put his tongue in my mouth. I involuntarily moaned as he dry-humped me right in the hallway, and I kissed him with the same passion, sucking his tongue and licking the inside of his mouth. His lips moved from mine and kissed across my jaw to my ear, then began to suck on my earlobe. He licked his lips and kissed the back of my ear. That's my spot and he knew it.

"Jameeellll," I softly moaned his name.

He lifted his head up to meet my eyes, then reached down to undo my belt buckle. I did the same, pulling his belt from the loops. We stared at each other as we popped buttons and unzipped zippers. He got there first, hooking his thumbs in the waistband of my pants and pulling them down with my boxer briefs, dropping to his knees as he did so. I put one hand on his head and the other on the wall and watched him blow me, my white-skinned cock fitting effortlessly in his mouth. I started moving with him, thrusting slightly into his mouth when he came toward me, letting him slide his brown full lips halfway down, tickling my slit with his tongue. His movements were unhurried. He didn't want to make me cum; he just wanted to make me want him.

When he had done enough, he stood and let his pants drop to the ground. He took off his Nikes and stepped out of the jeans, then took off his long-sleeved shirt, leaving his white tank top and underwear on. I touched his chest, noticeably bulkier than mine. I pinched one nipple through the fabric, and he made his whole pec flex then relax. I reached down and held his ten-inch cock through the cotton, an inch bigger and rounder than my own. As I began to rub him through his underwear, I bit one of his nipples through his thin tank top. He groaned. I did the same to the other one, and he lifted up his hands to run his fingers through my hair.

"Fuck me, Big Daddy," I commanded in a clear voice.

I saw the light dance in his eyes. He loved it when I called him Big Daddy. It was another corny name, but this one would never leave the bedroom.

Jamel stepped back, took my hand, and pulled me inside the bedroom. Once there, we kissed aggressively, grabbing onto each other, falling on top of the comforter. I rolled him onto his back, pulled off his tank top, and straddled him. I licked his razor bumps just below his chin. I sucked his Adam's apple and bit his neck hard. He groaned but allowed it. I made my way down, kissing his shoulder and his pecs, licking the tuft of hair in the center of his chest. I grazed my teeth through it, getting one or two hairs caught between my teeth. I sucked his little nubs and trailed my fingers down his abs. Jamel was in the gym at least twice a week, so his arms and legs are god-like, but my eight-pack beat his six-pack any day. I licked him there too, making my way down to my prize.

I pulled down his briefs and licked the cum oozing out. As I engulfed his cock, he moaned deeply and grabbed my hair roughly, then let go and ran his fingers through it instead. I bobbed up and down on his cock for a few moments and pumped with my hand a few moments more. He reached over to the nightstand and grabbed the lube, the jelly-like variety instead of the clear water-based one. This one was infused with ylang-ylang and ginseng, made for prolonging arousal. I smiled. *He wants to go at it for a while.* I took it from him and sat on the bed between his legs, my legs over his thighs, and he leaned back onto his elbows. I poured the cool gel in my hands and then rubbed them together. Then, I began to massage his dick.

I started at the base, upward strokes with one hand, a twist at his cock head, then back down again. I added my other hand to follow the first one and massaged up and down, twisting it around and around, adding pressure. He breathed faster, watching my hands instead of my eyes. My own cock was pointing straight up, leaking pre-cum. But I ignored it, focusing on pleasing my lover. After getting him nice and wet, I added more gel into my palm, then gently caressed his perfectly round testicles in my palm like Baoding balls. That drew louder moans from him. I stopped to add more gel, then moved my fingers downward to stroke his taint, then the outside of his hole.

I put two fingers in past the ring and he hissed. I looked up at him. "Want me to touch it?" I asked seductively.

He chuckled. "I thought you wanted me on top?"

"I do. But that doesn't mean I can't have a little fun too."

Jamel sat all the way up so that my fingers slid out. I held onto his cock with both hands. He picked up the lube off the bed and added it to his own hands. Then he reached over and grabbed my cock. He began stroking me hard and fast. I was a goner. My eyes quickly rolled back, and I forgot what I was doing. I fell backward onto my elbows and opened my legs wider. Then I couldn't take it and slid my body down toward him, silently letting him know I was ready. Jamel, never letting go of my cock, leaned up over me.

"How bad do you want it?" he asked in his quiet baritone.

"Fuck, Mel, just fuck me already," I said breathlessly.

He added gel to the tips of his fingers and pushed them inside my anus. As his three fingers made circles inside of me, he asked again, "How bad do you want it?"

I moaned loudly in response. He pulled his fingers out, leaving me feeling empty and unsatisfied. "Fuuuuuck, Mel."

He moved between my legs, and I instinctively lifted them up and held onto the back of my thighs. Jamel entered me slowly. I relaxed my body and let him in. When he bottomed out, my knees were tucked into his underarms. He pulled back halfway, and slowly slid inside me to the hilt. He did it again, and again, moving as smoothly as the ocean. The ridges of his steel cock grazed against my internal bundle of nerves. He expertly kept pressure on my prostate, keeping me full. I was absolutely going to cum first.

Ten strokes in and my body began to tremble. I wanted him to go faster, but he wanted to prolong the agony and pleasure for me. I hated it and I loved it. I dug my nails into his arms as my orgasm began to build. Suddenly, it washed over me like a tidal wave; my cock spurted thick globs of cum, landing right on my chest. He stopped moving, probably to stop himself from cumming too. Jamel's breath was just as labored as mine. He nuzzled his nose with mine and kissed my lips softly, then put his tongue in my mouth and licked me, soothing the electric orgasm with his romantic kisses. He absentmindedly began to move again, a quicker pace than our earlier slow crawl.

Gripping my waist, he began to pound into me. He pulled back farther and pushed in harder, making my body jolt upward with every thrust. My body was still sensitive from my climax, but I wanted this pounding from the moment we came into the house.

I started talking shit to him like I typically do. "Yeah! Beat this ass up! It's your man-pussy, baby. Fuck me harder, daddy, fuck me harder! You love this tight ass, don't you, baby! Fuck this pussy like you own it! Yeah, big daddy, fuck this hole like it's yours! Fuck me with your monster cock!"

He moved faster, losing his rhythm every now and again. I knew he was close. I started stroking myself. "Maybe I will cum again, big daddy! That cock gonna make me cum again? I know you can baby. Make me cum again. Fuck me, daddy, fuck me!"

He growled and pushed my knees into my chest. He fucked me harder, grunting with each thrust, his thighs slapping against my ass. I kept taunting him, calling out his name while stroking myself. I was so close. Finally, he pushed in, holding onto my ass as he delivered a series of shallow strokes. I felt his cock head swell, his semen warming me up from the inside. The feeling alone exhilarated me, and I moaned as I began to cum again, the second time within the hour, adding thinner ropes to my already painted chest.

"Fuck … me," I panted.

Mel chuckled as he slowly slid out of me and rolled onto his back. But my man likes to cuddle, so he pulled me close and turned on his side to drape his arm around my waist and his leg over mine. He lovingly kissed my shoulder, laid his cheek upon it, and sighed. I gently caressed the hairs on his arm as he held me. After a while, his light snores rumbled against me as his breath warmed my skin.

"I love you," I whispered to him in the dark. His breathing continued at a steady pace.

♥ • ♥ • ♥ CHAPTER 5 ♥ • ♥ • ♥

He's Your Goddamn Son.

~~~October 2012~~~

We invited The Major and Donny over for dinner on a Friday night, two weeks later. With Mama Denita spending all of her time at Ty's house, we offered to make a home-cooked meal for them. But it was really a chance for Donny to fess up to his father about his son. We weren't going to push him, but Jamel told him, "If there is an opportunity to do it right, this is it. So, take the opportunity."

Before the night began, I pulled Mel aside. "I'm just going to let you know, this is not my circus and not my monkeys. You got this, right? Because I have no idea what to expect, so I'm going to try very hard not to get involved. I'm just here for moral support."

He chuckled. "Yeah, I got it. But give me back up, just in case. Because I have no idea what to expect either. All I know is that my father has one heart attack under
~~~

him, and we aren't trying to cause a second. If one of them needs to leave the room, you're the escort."

"Deal," I said.

Donell did not show up high, thankfully. He was rarely high in his father's presence, but we were worried, nonetheless. We sat down to Jamel's perfectly grilled salmon with a pesto crust, seasoned green beans, and garlic bread. We don't have assigned seating at my house—something the both of us grew up with having military dads—but we offered The Major the head of the table anyway. He sat on one side and Donny sat directly across from him. Jamel and I sat on the same side.

We were casually eating, and Donny and I chatted about the Red Sox, the upcoming election, and Twitter, which was where everyone was going now for social media. Jamel, very much like his dad, wasn't very talkative so I was used to either eating in silence or carrying the conversation. Luckily, Donny was more like his mother and very talkative. He was nervous and needed to fill the air with words, so I was happy to give him that.

Eventually, Jamel cleared his throat and gave his brother a look, then continued eating. The Major caught the exchange. "What's going on?" he asked.

"Nothing, Pop," Donell said quickly. I could tell Jamel wanted to look up at him but didn't.

"Jamel?" Major Jones asked.

He sighed and looked at his father. "Nothing, sir. We're fine."

"Well, you don't look fine," his father said. "Is there something you want to tell me?"

Jamel looked confused. It dawned on me that when I spoke to The Major about being there for his sons, no matter what, he must have automatically assumed I meant Mel.

"I'm fine, sir," he said again.

"Okay," he said. "Because whatever it is, I can handle it. As long as it's the truth and the whole truth. If something happened that night when Connor's father came over that you left out before, I should know about it."

Shit, now he thinks we're the ones keeping secrets.

Jamel shook his head. "We're not keeping anything from you, Pop. You have my word."

The Major looked skeptical. He glanced at me, then back at Jamel, as if waiting for one of us to break. Donny cleared his throat.

"Um... Pop?" The Major turned his attention to his third son. "I do have something to tell you."

The Major pushed his plate away, clasped his hands together, and said calmly, "I'm listening."

Donell took a deep breath and let it out slowly. He sat up straighter in his chair and mimicked his father's hands on the table. "You remember my friend Vanessa? From Spellman?"

"Yes."

"Well. Vanessa and I never really stopped seeing each other when I moved back home. And in the midst of us seeing each other..." He paused for a moment, opened his mouth a few times, then just came out with it. "Vanessa became pregnant."

The Major had no reaction. He didn't move a muscle, didn't twitch his jaw, didn't even narrow his eyes. And all I could think was *Uh-oh*. Because the quieter Mel got, the angrier he was, and I could see his father being the same way. He stared at his son, who must have been trying very hard not to shrink under the table. But Donny kept his head high and pressed on.

"At the time, she thought she was going to have an abortion. I never influenced her decision in any way, and I told her I would be there for her whatever she decided. She decided to keep the baby."

I waited again and still … nothing. I glanced at Jamel out of my periphery, but he was watching Donny.

"We talked about getting married and ultimately decided that it was not the best thing for us to do. But we agreed to co-parent, and that's what I've been doing. Co-parenting with Vanessa. Since May 25th of this year."

Jamel's eyes wandered over to his father who still had not moved a muscle. The Major scared me on a typical day, but this non-reaction thing was making me want to crawl under the table.

"So… you see… I have a 4-month-old son … with Vanessa," Donny finished.

Then he went quiet. Even my dogs were quiet. We all waited to see what The Major's reaction was going to be, but he sat there for about twenty seconds, still as stone. He just stared at Donny, hardly blinking. Then, his gaze slowly wandered over to me.

It was intense under the gaze of The Major, but I held on, staring at him right back, reminding him what he told me: that whatever decisions we made, if we owned up to them, he would stand by us. His eyes glossed over at Jamel too, then slowly made their way back to Donny.

He looked down, unclasped his hands, flexed them, then clenched them into a tight fist. He repeated this several times before he reclasped his hands on the tabletop. Then he looked up at Donny. "How could you be so fucking stupid?" he said quietly.

And so, it begins.

"You were having unprotected sex with a woman you never had any intention of marrying. A black woman. Your first mistake. You get an educated black woman pregnant and derail her entire future all because you needed to fuck her raw. Your second mistake."

Hoooooly shit. I'd never really heard the Major curse before, let alone say the words, "fuck her raw."

"Then, you stupidly decided that your *feelings* were more important than your commitment and obligation to this woman whose life you've fucked up. You decided that the best course of action was not to make an honest woman out of her and marry her, but instead, make her into another statistic: a young, black, single mother. Did I get that right? Did I miss anything here, Donell?"

Donny was smart enough not to answer, and to his credit, he never shrank under his father's tongue lashing. I saw his Adam's Apple bob a few times but other than that, he just stared back at his father, who continued berating him.

"And then you kept this child from us because you're too much of a pussy to own up to the fact that you knocked up an educated black woman and made her a single mother. And it's all because you're too fucking stupid to wear a fucking condom."

He got silent again, then roared, "FOR FOUR FUCKING MONTHS!"

Holy. Shit. I'd never even heard The Major speak very loudly, let alone scream like that.

Jamel spoke quietly, "Pop—"

Major Wendel roared again, "SHUT THE FUCK UP!" He glared at Jamel who instantly shut his mouth. My eyes went wide but I said nothing. *Not my circus, not my monkeys.*

Then he turned his attention back to Donny. "And now your son—your SON—is going to grow up without a father in his life to teach him how to be a man, to—"

"He's not going to grow up without me," Donny boldly cut him off. "I told you, we're co-parenting."

The Major stood up and yelled again, "From 500 miles away!? I should knock the shit out of your stupid ass."

Donny raised his voice, which I thought was partly brave and partly stupid. "I'm down there every other weekend, and when I'm there, I take him. I hold him, I change him, I feed him, I wash him, I put him to sleep. And when he's old enough, he's going to spend time up here with ME."

"Yeah? Is that when you were planning on telling me? When you showed up one day at the house with a goddamn 12-year-old wanting to spend time with his absentee father!?"

"Pop, your heart," Jamel reminded him.

"Didn't I tell you to shut the fuck up?" The Major snapped. "You and Connor, you set this shit up, didn't you?"

"Major, sir," I answered, "we just wanted to give you and Donny the cha—"

"You don't get to fucking talk either, boy!" he snarled at me. "Since you're one of my stupid ass sons now, keeping secrets, fucking up your lives left and right, and leaving me to clean up your goddamn messes. You'd still be sitting in a jail cell if it wasn't for my connections with a top law firm, so you shut the fuck up too!"

That should have offended me, but it had the opposite effect. Yeah, he basically called me a fuck up and a dumbass, but he was also showing me a side of himself that he only shows to his immediate family. His sons. His outburst came from a place of love for his sons and disappointment in their choices, not because he despised who they were. It made me happy in a weird way. So yeah, I shut the fuck up too.

He turned back to Donny. "What exactly is your plan here? And please don't say another stupid thing like, 'we're co-parenting.' Because we both know that's not going to work. He needs a father, 24/7. She needs a partner, 24/7. That baby is crying right now. RIGHT. NOW. And you're not there to help her. What, she got her mother and sisters helping her? Maybe an 80-year-old grandmother somewhere? That's her support? A team of black women raising your fucking son while you sit here eating GODDAMN SALMON!?"

The Major slapped his entire plate onto the floor. I flinched as it crashed onto the hardwood. It reminded me of when my angry father would throw shit around. An ass whooping would follow, usually mine.

Jamel saw me flinch and stood up. "That's enough, Pop," he said sternly. "You made your point. Donny fucked up. What's done is done and the child is already here. Now we're going to sit here and try to figure out how we're going to make it right. That's why we set this up. This is where we help Donny put together a game plan, so that he can be an active father to his son."

I thought The Major was going to snap at Jamel for talking to him that way, for speaking at all. Instead, he pointed his finger at Donny. "Donell Matias Jones, you're going to stay in this child's life forever, do you understand me?"

"Yes sir, you don't even—"

"Shut the fuck up!" The Major yelled. Donny nodded.

"I don't care if you have a falling out, and she ends up hating you," the Major continued. "I don't give a shit if she marries someone else and has more children. That is *your* son, *your* responsibility, from now until the day you die. So even when he does stupid shit like get arrested for underage drinking or shoots someone or knock up some woman and destroys all her hopes and dreams, you get to tell him what a dumb fuck he is and he'll listen because he's *your* goddamn son. You stay in his life no matter what! Do you understand me?"

Poor Donny's eyes started pooling with tears and he nodded. "Answer me!" his father yelled again.

"Yes, sir," he choked out. He put his face in his hands and began to sob.

The Major was unmoved. He walked around the table and went to the front door. "I need air," he said quietly, right before he slammed it shut.

Donny put his face on the table and cried. Mel and I looked at each other with the obvious question: *Who takes on who?* Mel pointed his chin at Donny as if to say, *Stay with him.* Then he walked around the table and went to talk with his father. I sat in Jamel's chair, rubbing Donny's shoulders in an attempt to comfort him.

When his shoulders stopped shaking and his crying subsided, I said to him, "Hey, Donny, guess what?" He didn't answer but I didn't need him to. "I think your dad has fully accepted me as part of the family."

"What?" he asked from inside his arms.

"Your dad!" I said excitedly. "Didn't you hear how he included me in all that talk about his sons fucking up their lives? He was all like, 'Look at you: keeping secrets, and fucking up your life, and getting arrested for murder and shit, and now I have to clean up your goddamn messes like my other dumb ass sons, blah blah blah.'" I mimicked the Major's yelling voice.

Donny lifted his head up and looked at me, then he started laughing. Together, we laughed a bit madly. He wiped his eyes and we got quiet. "Well," he finally said, "that went better than I expected." We looked at each other and laughed again.

"Dude. The whole time in my head I'm like, 'Hoooooly shit, he's really laying into you, leaving it all on the table.' I know you all said it, but to be on the inside, watching it? I'm sorry but it was a thing of beauty. When he yelled at Jamel, 'Shut the fuck up!,' man, I think my heart stopped." I touched my chest dramatically.

Donny chuckled. "Shit, I thought he was going to throw his plate at my head."

"Shit, I thought so too!"

When our laughter died down, I put my hand on his shoulder again. "You did good, Don. I'm proud of you. You were honest, you stood up for yourself, defended your decisions, and didn't back down."

"Then I cried like a baby," he said with a smile.

I smiled back. "Listen, my father used to put me in a straight jacket and cave my chest in. The fact that your father called you stupid a couple a times, a pussy once, and made you cry without putting his hands on you, I'd say he's doing an alright job."

"Damn, Con," he said sadly. "If that's the bar, then he's doing a fantastic job."

"My thoughts exactly." I patted his back. "You okay though?"

"Yeah. Yeah, I'm okay." He sniffed. "Thank you, Connor. I'm glad you're my brother."

I smiled and patted his back again. "I'm glad to have little brothers."

The door opened and Jamel and Major Jones came in. Donny abruptly stood and so did I. Jamel came over to the seat that I had occupied and stood next to the chair. The Major went to stand at the head of the table. He looked at each of us as we waited silently. "What's my grandson's name?" he finally asked.

"DJ. Donell Matias Robinson, Junior."

"He's not a junior if he doesn't have your last name," the Major told him. "You get the birth certificate changed immediately."

"Yes, sir."

The Major sighed, then sat down. We sat down after him. "Okay. I'm listening. What's the plan?"

CHAPTER 6

My Family Is Already Being Torn Apart

~~~December 2012~~~

I found it telling that my trial officially started on December 6, the same day I came home from the Marine Corps for good back in 2006. That day was extremely emotional for me because all I wanted to do was come home after losing Vinnie three months prior. My life started over that day. Whatever the outcome, I knew this trial was going to change my life forever.

I wore a black suit and held hands with Jamel as we headed up the court steps to meet Kelly, my attorney, his second-chair, a young lawyer named Barron Joseph, and Major Jones. "Nothing is really going to happen today but preliminary stuff," Kelly explained. "We meet the jury and go through a couple of motions,
~~~

revealing our official witness list. If we have time, we'll do opening remarks."

"Who is testifying for my dad?" I asked.

Kelly hesitated. "Benjamin Jennings, Sr. Your dad's best friend?"

"Of course. BJ and Sam's dad. A bigot just like him. Who else?"

"A couple of nurses and the doctor that operated on him. Detective Gram, who interviewed you both. A couple of other people."

"My mom?" That's what I really wanted to know.

"No," said Kelly. "Your mom can't be compelled to testify for or against her own husband. Your sister Angela is already a witness for you. As far as I know, Mary Kate is not taking the stand for either side. But your brother…"

"He's testifying against me," I finished for him. "Siding with my father. What a shocker."

"Listen, Connor—"

He started to talk, but we were all distracted by my father coming up the stairs holding my mother's hand tightly. He glared at me like he wanted to wring my neck. Matty trailed behind them, holding his wife Stephanie's hand. Mary Kate was last, wearing a black dress and hat like she was going to a funeral. My mother glanced at me but then looked away.

"Do I need to—" I began to ask.

"No, you're with me," Kelly said. "They will go right inside."

We all turned to watch them walk past us, but Mary Kate broke rank and walked over to me. My family paused at the doorway to watch her. She reached up, and I leaned down so that she could hug me. We held each other for a long moment, not needing to speak. I knew she loved me and our family, and this whole thing was killing her inside. I pulled back first.

"Go with them," I quietly said. I was not going to make her choose.

She nodded, her eyes welling up. But she turned to walk back to them. Matty put his arm around her and smirked at me before they disappeared behind the glass doors.

Judge Gabriel Wood was presiding over the case. Barron said he had only been on the bench for about eight years. He was known to be no nonsense, yet fair. His rulings never leaned liberal or conservative; he followed the law to the letter. You just never knew what you were going to get.

Kelly was right. It was a lot of legal jargon. Some of it I understood, some of it went over my head. I was to keep silent and look innocent for the jury. Angie, who was studying to be a lawyer, could not miss her first class but slid in next to Jamel around 11:30 a.m. She pointedly ignored our family. Lots of motions were filed and passed. One of Merchant's expert witnesses got dismissed after Kelly's team found out she had disowned a gay cousin. Jack was dismissed too. Merchant alleged that our previous romantic relationship, his previous interactions with the law, heated interactions with my father and Ethan where Ethan almost beat the shit out of him, and Jack actually beating the shit out of my brother, made him a biased witness. The judge called it at 2 p.m. for lunch and then decided to just end the session for the day. Tomorrow would begin with opening statements.

I let my family walk out first, then took Jamel's hand and walked out behind them. I saw my mother turn around and heard my father snap, "Where are you going, Katherine?"

"To the bathroom, dear. I'll be out in a jiff."

"Don't take too long," he said gruffly.

She walked past us and didn't look in our direction at all. But as soon as my father and siblings passed through the revolving doors, I let go of Jamel's hand and turned to follow her.

"Connor," Jamel warned quietly. I ignored him. "Connor," he called my name a little louder, drawing the attention of my attorney.

"Where's he going?" Kelly asked Jamel. But Jamel didn't answer him. My partner already knew.

I watched my mother enter the bathroom with the figure of a woman on the door and walked in behind her. She pretended to be startled by my intrusion. I stared at her, then turned around and locked the door. That's when she began to cry.

She kept repeating, "I'm so sorry, I'm so sorry, I'm so sorry."

I put my arms around her. "It's okay, Mom. It's okay."

I held her until her sniffles stopped. "You have to let me go," she said.

I knew I needed to. She was going to pay big time for this. I was sure he figured it out already why she delayed herself. But I needed to hold onto my mother just a moment longer. And apparently, she felt the same because she didn't let me go either.

She touched my face. "No matter what happens, I will always love you. My amazing and beautiful gay son. I love you, Connor."

And that was what made the tears fall out of my eyes too. I grabbed her in a hug and cried on her shoulder. She became the one comforting me, rubbing my back as I murmured, "I'm so sorry. I didn't mean for this to happen. I'm so sorry, Mom."

"I have to go," she reminded me.

"I love you, Mom," I responded.

She let me go first. I stood by the door and watched her transform herself back into Owen McIntyre's wife. She went over to the sink and washed her face, then patted her cheeks dry with a paper towel. She reapplied her lipstick and put eyedrops in her eyes to get some of the red out. She adjusted her clothes and walked to the door.

Before she opened it, my mother pulled my face down to kiss my cheek, leaving a red lipstick smudge behind.

"I love you, Connor," she whispered. Then, she was gone.

We spent that week and the next watching Merchant parade a bunch of doctors and nurses through the courtroom. They explained how I almost killed my father, that if the bullet was inches to the right or left it would have shattered an artery. Kelly was good. He let the doctors say what they needed to say about my father's medical condition, then in cross examination, he asked about his demeanor. "How did he appear? Sad? Heartbroken?" They could only say that he was more angry than anything else.

Three of my father's lodge members praised him as a hardworking man and a loving and devoted father that would do anything for his children. They all said variations of the same thing: How I was straight my whole life and they don't know what happened to me. Kelly didn't even bother questioning them. The witnesses implied that Afia pushed Jamel on me. I was glad she wasn't in the courtroom to hear that. Lovie wasn't coming to court until the prosecution rested; she didn't want to hear any of the negative stuff about me. But Jack was there, right next to Jamel, and so was Angie, every day.

Ben Jennings Sr. was the prosecution's most compelling witness because he knew us intimately. In his heavy Irish accent, he talked about my father's strong family values, Christian beliefs, morals, and ethics. He described his love for his children, especially the son that followed in his footsteps and served like he did. He talked about me as a boy and how I had an active sex life with females. Apparently the whole town knew it. Even after I came home from the military, I was seen in the company of women, especially my high school sweetheart, Afia. He'd seen us kiss and hug on several occasions and said that if I was turned gay, it was not my fault, but the devils around me. I knew he meant Jack. *Fuck him for that.*

Kelly stood up and asked him flat out, "How do you feel about homosexuality?"

"I don't feel any kind of way about it," he said nonchalantly. "I try not to think about it at all."

"But don't you have a gay nephew? Your brother's son in Albania, Christopher Jennings?" Kelly challenged him.

Mr. Jennings did not like that being brought up at all. "I do," he said curtly.

"How do you get along with him?"

"We don't see each other. He lives in Europe."

"But he was here recently, was he not? Came to visit your sister Lacey; your children, Moira, Ben Junior, and Samuel; and other friends in the Rockville area. He came with his husband Ciaran Beals."

Kelly paused for a long while, long enough to make Mr. Jennings visibly uncomfortable. I wondered if Chris had visited Jack. I knew he was Jack's first love. The thought made me happy for Jack, but I didn't turn around to look at him.

"He did not visit you," Kelly continued. "Your brother's only son. Why was that?"

"We don't talk much."

"You don't talk much, or you don't talk at all?"

Mr. Jennings hesitated, then said, "We don't talk at all."

"Is it because he's gay?"

"Objection!" Merchant roared.

"Overruled," the judge said. "You may answer the question."

Mr. Jennings looked away and said, "It's because we do not see eye to eye on issues."

"Issues pertaining to his lifestyle."

"Yes."

"His *homosexual* lifestyle."

He paused then said, "Among other things."

Kelly nodded, pacing the room. "Isn't it true that you threatened your children that if they flew to Albania and attended his wedding to his now husband, they would lose their inheritance money?"

Mr. Jennings looked up sharply. "Objection! Where are you getting this information!?" Merchant yelled.

"I have it on good authority these statements to be true from members of his own family."

"Well, Mr. Jennings is not on trial. Your murderous client is," he retorted nastily.

"How DARE y—"

The judge banged his gavel a couple of times. "ENOUGH! Mr. Kelly, move this questioning along."

"Yes, Your Honor." Kelly turned back to the older man. "Is it safe to assume that you have strong opinions about the gay lifestyle?"

"You can assume that," Mr. Jennings replied.

Kelly smiled. "Is it safe to assume that your friend and ally Owen McIntyre shares similar views and values concerning this issue?"

"Objection!" Merchant yelled again. "He can't speak to my client's values."

"But he has been speaking to your client's values for the last hour, hasn't he?" Kelly looked at the jury. "He has talked about his Christian values, family values, and their close friendship. If there is anyone in this room, other than Mr. McIntyre's own dear wife, that can speak to his values, certainly it would be his best friend, no?"

Merchant began to speak but the judge cut him off. "I'll allow it. Briefly."

Kelly turned his attention back to Mr. Jennings. "Have you and Staff Sergeant McIntyre had conversations relating to gays in the military?"

Mr. Jennings glanced at my father. "We have."

"And do you share similar values and views around this topic?"

He swallowed, then said, "We agree that it is a distraction from the mission to have men who lie with men sharing bunks and breaking bread with regular men."

Kelly looked at the jury again. "'Regular men,' you say? So gay men aren't regular men? Are they men at all to you?"

"Objection! Leading!" the ADA called out.

"Withdrawn." Kelly looked back at Mr. Jennings. "In your opinion, how should men who lie with men be treated? Locked away? Stoned? What is your biblical truth around this issue?"

Ben shrugged. "It's not my call. The Lord will deal with them soon enough."

Kelly nodded. "Including Corporal McIntyre? And his male lover and partner, Jamel Jones? Will the Lord deal with them too?"

Ben Jennings turned to look at me. It was the first time he looked at me since he came into the courtroom. Unlike my father, there wasn't hate in his eyes for me. It was the look you give to the help, if you look at them at all. I was beneath him, not even worthy to be in the same room. "The Lord will deal with them soon enough," he repeated.

Kelly let his words hang in the air. Then he said, "Like how your friend Owen tried to deal with his own son?"

"Objection!" the ADA called out again.

"Withdrawn," he said lazily. "One more question. You're a proud gun owner, correct? A card-carrying member of the NRA?"

"I am," Mr. Jennings said proudly.

"Glad to hear it. So, you must believe strongly in Stand Your Ground laws, correct? The right to defend your home and property?"

"Yes, I do."

"Do you consider yourself a pretty good marksman?"

"I am," he said again proudly.

"And if someone came into your home and threatened your family, what would you do?"

"I would defend my home and family."

"With your legally registered firearm?"

"If it came to that, yes."

"Didn't it come to that? About ten years ago?" Kelly walked over to the table and Barron handed him a sheaf of papers. "Police report," he explained, handing out copies to the jury. He handed Mr. Jennings one too. "Can you tell us what happened the night of March 20, 2003?"

Mr. Jennings' eyes narrowed at my attorney. "I had an intruder in my house."

"Your daughter's boyfriend? Didn't she let him in the home?"

"He was still an intruder."

"What made him an intruder?"

"Because I am the homeowner, and I didn't want him there. I told him to leave, and he didn't."

"What did you do?"

"I fired a warning shot."

Kelly raised his eyebrow. "A warning shot in his leg?"

"Yes. I just wanted him to know that I meant business."

Kelly strolled over to the jury box. "Someone came into your home uninvited, you asked him to leave, and he didn't. You fired a warning shot that ended up in his leg because you wanted him to know you were serious, not because you actually wanted to kill the boy. Did I get that right?"

Stupidly, he just figured out the correlation. Even Merchant couldn't help him out of this one. "That's correct," he said in a low voice.

"And being the marksman that you are, you could have killed him, but you know the difference between a warning shot and a kill shot, is that right?"

"That's ... right."

"So, in your own opinion, if someone came into Corporal Connor McIntyre's home that he didn't want to be there, that he considered an intruder, that threatened his home and family, and refused to leave, did Corporal McIntrye have the right as a legally registered gun owner and homeowner to fire a warning shot and defend his home and family?"

Merchant tried to shut it down. "Objection! Mr. Jennings is not an expert!"

"I asked for his opinion, not his expertise, as someone who has been through a similar situation," Kelly said simply.

The judge considered it. "You may answer the question, Mr. Jennings."

Mr. Jennings glared at Kelly, but then said, "I suppose so."

"Uh-huh, so I suppose the Corporal's response is not so far-fetched from any other ... *regular* man."

"Was that a question!?" Merchant asked loudly.

"No, it wasn't," Kelly said with a smug smile. "The defense rests."

He walked over and sat in his seat. Kelly knew he nailed the bastard and so did Merchant.

❤

The next day, my brother was the first witness. Like Mr. Jennings, he got on the stand and sang my father's praises. It was upsetting to watch, but I kept my face straight and listened to him talk about how wonderful our childhood was, how our father taught us how to shoot and hunt, and instilled family and Christian values in us. How he was the best father in the world. How disappointed he was to hear that I had "taken up with a man," as he put it. That it was not like me at all; the war had changed me. He even threw in how much I loved Afia and how great she was for me, which was surprising since he spit on her and Jack beat the shit out of him for it. He told the courtroom that Afia was my one true love, not some man that had brainwashed me. I hated him for that.

Before he began his cross-examination, Kelly said in a low voice, "Connor, I need you to know: first I'm going to break him down. Then I'm going to bury your brother in perjury charges."

"I don't give a shit, Kelly. Bury that asshole," I said quietly back.

Kelly stood up. "Matthew … or Matty? How should I address you, sir?" he asked respectfully.

"Matty is fine," my stupid ass brother said, as if he had some authority over him.

Kelly nodded. He walked over to the witness stand. "Did your father ever physically abuse you, Matty?"

"No," he answered automatically. "My father used corporal punishment to discipline us, but it wasn't abuse. I wouldn't be the man I am today without my father's stern discipline, just the way God intended. I am thankful for him, every day."

Kelly nodded again. "Did that stern discipline include belt buckle beatings, fists to the chest and stomach, kicks to the groin, chokeholds, and straitjackets?"

The jury looked horrified. Merchant yelled, "Objection!"

"Overruled," the judge said right away. I think he wanted to know too. "Answer the question."

Matty took a moment and said, "If he did, I don't remember. I wasn't someone who was disciplined often. I did what I was told and followed the rules."

"Okay. What do you remember about the abuse?"

"Objection," Merchant said. "He already said he wasn't abused. Nice try, Counselor."

"Withdrawn," Kelly said with a hand wave. "Matty, when was the last time you were … sternly disciplined?"

"I don't remember," he said with a shrug.

"You don't remember…" Kelly walked back over to the table and again, Barron was waiting for him. He handed Kelly a stack of documents, keeping a copy for himself. I looked over at the document; Matty had no idea what was coming. Kelly handed out copies to the jurors and then to Matty.

"Matty, what happened the night of May 29, 1997? A week after your 16th birthday."

I watched the color drain from my brother's face as his mouth opened slightly, reading the hospital discharge papers. My spineless brother lied through his teeth, as he always did. "I was attacked by Hispanic gang members in Providence and ended up in the hospital for five days."

"Matty," Kelly said with a bit of pity creeping into his tone. "I think we both know that's not what happened."

"Is that a question!?" Merchant yelled.

Matty shook his head. "That's what happened. I filed a police report."

Kelly walked toward him, getting aggressive with every word. "So, your father didn't *beat* you with fists, *breaking* your nose and several teeth, *dislocating* your jaw—"

"Objection!" Merchant yelled.

"—broke two ribs and bruised five more—"

"Objection! Your Honor!" Merchant stood up as Kelly kept going.

"—sprained neck, grade-two concussion—"

The judge banged his gavel. "Enough, Mr. Kelly."

"—almost obliterated your kidney to where it had to be removed—"

"Objection, he is badgering my witness!" Merchant cried again.

Kelly ignored the two of them. "Your father didn't attempt to kill you? All because you tried to physically stop him from abusing your 8-year-old little sister who he slammed against the wall and slapped until her nose ran with blood, repeatedly in the face eleven times—"

The judge banged his gavel again. "Enough, Counselor."

"Eleven times, Matty!" He began to slap his hands together as he counted: "One! Two! Three! Four! Five!"

The judge banged his gavel six times, "Enough, Counselor! You made your point!"

By this time, Kelly was right up against the witness stand and my brother was definitely rattled. His teeth were glued together, his lips parted. His eyes were glassy, almost like he was reliving the incident. He clenched his fists so tightly his knuckles were white. It was silent in the courtroom as we all waited.

"Matty?" Kelly called his name softly. "Did your father ever physically abuse you?"

It took him a moment, but Matty's eyes slowly moved over to my father. I couldn't help but to look over there as well. Owen was stone-faced, but he gave my brother the look. The look that said, *You talk, you die.* I realized that Matty was still pinned under my father's thumb. He would lie and go to jail before he admitted to anything that happened that night.

Matty pulled his bottom lip in to wet it, then, with just as much conviction as he did the first time, said, "I wouldn't be the man I am today without my father's stern discipline. Just the way God intended. And I am thankful to him, every day."

Except, this time, a tear rolled down his cheek. He quickly wiped it away.

"Well, let's just hope and pray that you aren't giving your son the same kind of God-intended discipline that you got, eh?" Kelly replied.

"Fuck you," Matty spat.

Merchant shouted his objection at the same time the judge banged his gavel. "Don't worry, I'm done here," Kelly said as he walked back to the table, shaking his head.

Matty sat there a moment longer but then got off the stand. He glared at me with hatred as he walked out of the courtroom. I was busy staring him down when Barron spoke. "You should add the sister to the list. Subpoena her," he said to Kelly.

"What!?" My attention snapped to my attorneys.

"Your sister. Mary Kate," said Barron. "When Kelly started berating Matty, she walked out of the court-room. She did it quietly, but I saw her. She was crying. She'll talk. She could be the smoking gun."

"No." There was no way I was going to let MK relive that fateful night.

Kelly started, "Connor—"

"NO!" I raised my voice louder than I intended, drawing the attention of a couple of jurors. I took a deep breath and said, "You leave Mary Kate and my mother out of all of this, or I will fire you both and represent myself."

"This isn't the movies. No one does that in real life, Connor," Barron said condescendingly.

"Except me. I will. My family is already being torn apart. She stays out of this. Do you both hear me? Do you!?"

"It's fine, Connor. Angie is going to testify on your behalf. Mary Kate isn't getting subpoenaed," Kelly agreed.

"Thank you," I said curtly. I looked behind me and caught Jamel's eyes. He had heard the exchange, and he nodded in agreement.

I'm Here To Support Connor.

After my brother's testimony, the prosecution rested, so it was our turn. I guess they weren't going to let Owen take the stand and sink himself, which was fine by me. I planned on taking the stand, telling my side of the story.

Kelly started with his opening statements, basically summarizing my abusive childhood, how I'd grown from the mistakes I'd made, how I was a fine young man. He discussed my skillset as a Marine and reiterated over and over again that if I wanted my father dead, he would have died.

The first witness Kelly called was C.O. Master Sergeant Berganot. He was a good choice because he had seen me at every step of my military career. He came in in full uniform and commanded respect. The Master Sergeant talked about my time on base and deployment in Iraq. That I wasn't just a decorated Marine but a leader in all areas. He was the one who approved me for Lance Corporal, then Corporal. He spoke about my work, my team, my ethics, my values, and my love of country. He spoke about me not just as a Marine but as a human. Kelly got him to talk about my skill, how sharp I was, why I was chosen to lead a Fire Squad, and that anyone I wanted to kill stayed dead. Based on his understanding and expertise, I was not trying to kill my father. His testimony was perfect. So perfect that Merchant didn't conduct a cross examination. When Berganot came off the stand, he walked toward me, and I instinctively stood up. He saluted me and I saluted back. Then he walked out of the courtroom, assumingly back to Camp Lejeune in New River, North Carolina.

Taylor testified the next day. Joe, Simon, and Benjin sat in the pew behind Jamel, Jack, Angie, and Afia, who began coming to court. Out of the four men in my unit, Taylor was the one that Kelly decided should testify on my behalf. Instead of having all four talk and say similar things, he wanted to just have one person talk about my character, my leadership, and my morals. Of all of them, Taylor could speak to who I was on a personal level.

There wasn't a hint of the playful Taylor on the stand. He was serious, even when he talked about how fun and lively I was. But Taylor also spoke about the abuse I experienced because I confided in him as early as basic training. Merchant tried to object, but the judge shut him down. Taylor told the court everything that I told him about the beatings and how he offered to have me stay with him when it was time to leave the Marine Corps, so that I would never have to go back home again. He was believable.

He talked about the people we lost, including Vinnie, and how that triggered all of us so badly that one by one we left the Marines and compelled us to start Vinnie's Vet Buddies. That was the first time my family understood why I left. Like Kelly did with my C.O., he made sure to let it be known, once again, how good of a shot I was; if I wanted to kill my father, he would be dead.

Merchant cross-examined and tried to trip him up. But Taylor was adamant that I reported my physical abuse, repeated details that I gave to him, including my brother's near-death experience. Then Merchant really screwed up. "Connor didn't have any female romantic interests while in the Marines?" he asked.

Taylor shrugged. "I didn't see any females around."

"Was that because he was waiting to come home and rekindle his relationship with his high school sweetheart Afia?"

Taylor shook his head. "No. Connor was in love with someone else."

My mouth dropped. I shook my head, but Taylor wouldn't look at me. "He can't... he can't..." I whispered.

"He can. I told him to," Kelly said without looking at me.

I didn't understand. But before I could ask why, Merchant's curiosity got the best of him, and he fell right into Kelly's trap. "Who was Connor in love with?"

"A private on base. A male private. Connor was in love with another man."

That got the attention of every single person in the courtroom who didn't know about Vinnie and me, which excluded a total of seven people.

"You're making that up," Merchant said with a sneer. He turned to the judge. "Your Honor, remind the witness of his duty to be forthright with—"

Taylor raised his right hand. "Hand to God, Connor was in a romantic relationship with another man on base. I witnessed it with my own two eyes. So did all those fine people right there." He pointed to my unit. "He didn't become gay because of Army Sergeant Jamel Jones. He was already gay."

"Do you have any proof of this, Mr. Matherson?"

"Just my own eyes, the words from his own mouth, and the words of the private in question."

"And just who is this private?"

My mouth opened again and my heart hammered, afraid that my bullshit was going to out the man I loved. This would be a matter of public record, and then the world would know who Vinnie was to me. What he was. I wasn't ready for that, not before I prepared his widow Bethany and their son Leo.

But Taylor surprised everyone by saying, "I will not reveal his name. I don't want to tarnish the reputation of another Marine."

"Oh, you don't get to do that!" Merchant practically snarled at him. "You don't get to just magically pull out a gay Marine that Connor was supposedly sleeping with and not provide us with his name so we can question him ourselves. Unless it was you!?"

"It was not me," Taylor said plainly.

"Or one of your men here!?" Merchant gestured toward my unit.

Taylor shook his head. "It was not any one of those men sitting behind you. And again, I will not reveal his name."

"Your Honor!" Merchant cried.

"I'm sorry, young man, but you did bring it up. You will need to reveal his name," the judge said.

Taylor turned toward the judge. "And with all due respect, Your Honor, you have no idea how hard it is for gay, lesbian, transgender, and non-binary individuals in the military, even now after Don't Ask, Don't Tell was repealed. The last thing I will ever do is cause more hardship for a fellow Marine. If you find him, then you are more than welcome to have him sit in my spot and let him tell you himself. All I can tell you is that there was a real, solid, loving, and monogamous relationship between Connor and another man for almost two years."

"You are running the risk of being called into contempt," the judge warned.

"And I will happily take that risk, Your Honor. I will sit in jail and pay whatever fine, all to keep a fellow brother-in-arms safe. But I'm going to hope that you are an understanding judge who can be empathetic to my situation here. I'm here to support Connor. I'm not here to out another man."

To the ADA's dismay, the judge seemed to consider what Taylor was saying. "Your Honor! You can't possibly—"

The judge banged his gavel. "Are you done with your line of questioning, Counselor?"

The ADA was beside himself. He kept opening and closing his mouth. "Yes," he finally said through gritted teeth.

He went back to his seat and Kelly jumped up. "Redirect?"

"Go on," Judge Wood allowed.

Kelly strolled over to the witness booth. "Without revealing the name, can you tell us anything about the nature of their relationship?"

Taylor described the hidden love I shared with Vinnie, how close we were, both friends and lovers. How we both came from conservative families and leaned on each other, and we never thought we would ever see the day when we could be out. Don't Ask, Don't Tell made it impossible. We were committed to the oath we took to defend our country, and we didn't want our relationship to get in the way of our service. Taylor described how devastated I was when it ended, leaving out *how* it ended. He spoke of Vinnie in the present tense, as if he was still here on this earth with us. And maybe, somehow, he was.

"Thank you, Taylor. I appreciate your time here today."

Taylor came off the stand. As he passed me, he mouthed, "I'm sorry."

I mouthed back, "It's okay. Thank you." He resumed his seat next to the others.

❤

We broke for lunch and next up was my sister, Angela. She couldn't attest to the physical abuse because she had never seen it. But she could speak to my father's verbal, mental, and emotional abuse because he did it to all of us. She spoke of my father's bad temper, the way he would throw things and shake my mother if the house wasn't neat enough or if dinner was one minute late. She described his ridiculous, expletive-laden sermons: the girls were bitches and cunts; the boys were worthless pieces of shit. She remembered me wearing a straitjacket when I was a teen, having to stand in the corner for hours while she wasn't allowed to talk to me.

She spoke of the things he would say about Afia. He hated our relationship even more than I thought. She overheard him refer to her as my nigger girlfriend to our mother or brother on many occasions. I knew it hurt Afia to hear that.

I turned and caught Afia's eye as my sister continued. Ty was holding her hand. Before I could say anything, she whispered, "It's okay, it's okay." She put her fingers to her lips, kissed them, and sent it to me, making me smile. I turned back and noticed some jurors had witnessed the exchange. It was probably the first time they saw me smile since the trial began.

Angie spoke of the two incidents this year, the first when Jack and Ethan came to dinner at my family's home back in February. How Afia revealed that she was getting married to someone else after yelling at everyone that they had no idea who I really was, which led Angie to suspect there was something dubious about our relationship. How she came to my home where I admitted that I was gay and Jamel was my life partner. Angie spent the next couple of months hanging out with us and described the nature of our relationship firsthand: loving, playful, honest, real. Mutual.

The second incident was my drunken admission of my sexuality at her birthday party. She described the event in detail: my argument with our brother; our father forgetting himself and almost attacking me; BJ coming to my rescue; and my tears as Afia, Jack, and Liam comforted me. Her testimony was compelling because it was the complete opposite of Matty's.

But she also said something else. She was at the house that day, watching my father drink and talk on the phone with someone who was basically egging him on to get his son back, by force if necessary.

"I asked my mother who he was talking to, but she did not answer. Instead, I watched her hide my father's two handguns in the trash bin, the one he kept in the car and the one he kept in the bedroom. My mother broke the key in the door to the den, so he wouldn't have access to his other firearms. When he got off the phone, he went looking for them. When he realized what she did, he slapped her. It was the first time I saw my father hit my mother. I jumped between them, and he pushed me to the ground and called me a stupid cunt. Then he left the house. Again, I asked my mother what was going on. She didn't answer me; she just sat at the kitchen table and cried. When she did speak, the only thing she said was, 'Connor can take care of himself.' I tried to call my brother to warn him, but he didn't pick up the phone. I got in my car and drove over there, but by the time I did, everything had already happened."

"Who did it seem like he was talking to before he left?" Kelly asked.

"If I had to guess, I would say Ben Jennings, his bigoted best friend."

"Objection," Merchant called. "She has no way of knowing that."

The judge agreed. "Sustained. The jury will disregard."

Kelly let it go and changed tactics. "Your father was drinking?"

"Yes."

"And he was angry."

"Very."

"And he physically hit your mother and pushed you."

"Yes."

"And he left the home in a rage, seemingly to head over to Connor's home."

"That's what it seemed like to me."

"And what do you think he intended to do?"

"Objection!" Merchant cried.

"You know better, Kelly," the judge said sternly.

"Withdrawn," Kelly said with a nod. "What is your relationship like with your father now?"

"Well, he threw me out of the house, saying I chose sides. But I didn't choose sides. I just chose to support my brother who needed me. I will always choose my family."

"I'm sorry to hear that. Where are you staying?"

"Connor put me in an apartment at The Starling Residence, and Jamel is paying my rent. Thank God my tuition is already paid up this year or I'm pretty sure he would have stopped the check on that too. My father can be cruel when he wants to be."

"Thank you for your time today, Angie. I know this is hard for you." Kelly sat down and Merchant immediately stood up.

"Angela—or may I call you Angie?"

"You may call me *Miss* McIntyre," she said curtly.

The ADA smiled. "Ms. McIntyre. It's very evident that you love your brother Connor, yes?"

"Yes, I do."

"And you love your brother, Matthew?"

"I do."

"More or less or…" He raised an eyebrow.

"I love them both. I don't *like* my brother Matty right now, and I am hurting that my brother Connor is being accused of attempted murder, but I love both of my brothers."

He nodded. "And your father? Do you love your father?"

"With all my heart. But I'm mad at him too."

Merchant asked, "Do you believe your father loves Connor?'"

"I think…" She sighed. "My father loves the best way he knows how to love. I think he has a hard time accepting Connor for who he is."

"And who is that, Angie? Who is Connor?"

"Miss McIntyre," she corrected him. "Connor is a Marine vet, a mentor, leader, and friend, who just happens to be a gay man."

"His sexuality is not on trial—"

"But isn't it!?" Angie shrieked. "Isn't that why my father went to Connor's house that night? Isn't that why we're all here? Because of some illusion that Connor was suddenly hoodwinked into a same-sex relationship and all my father was trying to do was 'get him out'?" She put the last three words in air quotes. She looked directly at our father. "How could you do this? You're willing to send your own son to prison all because you can't accept that he's gay!?"

"Please do not direct your comments to my client," the ADA said as he stepped in front of her vision.

But it didn't stop her from yelling, tears sprouting from her eyes. "Let him go, Dad! Drop this whole thing and let him go! Please! You're tearing this family apart!" Owen kept his face as still as stone.

"Your Honor, please." Merchant looked to the judge for help.

"Young lady," Judge Wood said sternly. "Calm your-self down."

Angie put her head in her hands and sobbed. Merchant sighed. "No further questions."

Angie came off the stand. As she passed, she reached out her hand and our fingers touched. Then, she took her seat next to Jamel. He wrapped his arms around her and let her cry into his shoulder. Matty scowled at them.

"Call your next witness," the judge stated.

"The defense calls Liam Ferguson to the stand."

I turned around to watch Liam come to the front of the courtroom. Somehow, it had been decided that Liam would speak in Jack's place. He could probably attest to the relationship I had with Jack although he never actually saw us together. I always had a suspicion that Liam knew.

After he was sworn in and said his full name for the record, Kelly asked Liam about what he knew of my childhood since we were teammates and friends. Liam acknowledged that I had a lot of girlfriends and slept with most of them. But I learned something new from him too. When Kelly asked him when he realized that I wasn't straight, his answer shocked me.

"One day, toward the end of my freshman year, when Connor was a sophomore, we were sitting on a table at the Knoll—that's the area outside the cafeteria when we were able to eat outside—and Afia and Jack were passing by. I was sitting next to Connor when he called Afia over and Jack came with her. I don't remember what they were talking about, but I watched the way he looked at Jack. He got a little flustered, like how you get when you're around someone you have a crush on. After that, I started paying more attention to him when Jack was around. Jack started a relationship that summer with Chris Jennings, and I think it was kind of bittersweet for Connor because suddenly Jack was always around but also, he was completely unavailable.

"He became a bit of a mess, just all over the place from moody to giggly. It was kind of amazing to watch," Liam said with a chuckle. "I mentioned it to Jack, and he laughed me off, but I think he started paying attention too. So, it wasn't surprising to me at all that when Chris left and Jack came out to everyone officially, Connor was the first person to approach him."

I was pretty sure my entire face and neck was red. I imagined Jack was probably as red as I was, but I didn't dare turn around. I always wondered how Jack knew I was into him, and now I knew Liam was the culprit.

Liam continued discussing my secret relationship with Jack and how confused I was, based on the conversations he had with Jack during that time and how I kept sleeping with other girls. But he always knew when Jack and I broke up, because every time we did, I would be lost without him. Which was probably true.

"How old was Connor during this time?" Kelly asked.

"Connor was sixteen, Jack was fifteen when they began a relationship. It ended a year later. They had a big blow out over Connor teasing Jack in front of the entire baseball team about being gay. It hurt him tremendously. Jack said he couldn't do it anymore; he couldn't pretend like he wasn't in love with Connor while Connor pretended like they weren't in a relationship."

"Based on your observations, what was your assessment of Connor's sexuality?"

"Whatever Connor was during our teenage years, he wasn't straight. He was in love with Jack and Jack was in love with him."

Wow. He was spot on. I couldn't help but to smile, grateful for Liam.

"So why do you think Connor didn't come out as a teenager?" Kelly asked.

"I didn't know back then, but I understand now that Connor was terrified of his father's reaction. When Connor came out at the restaurant, I saw how his father looked at him. There was murder in his eyes."

"Objection! Seriously!?" Merchant yelled.

"Jury will disregard," the judge immediately said. "Mr. Ferguson, try not to make conjectures and just speak in terms of facts or your own observations."

Liam nodded respectfully at the judge, then he addressed the jury. "Well, the fact is, if BJ did not stand in front of Connor that night in the restaurant, his father would have absolutely beat the shit out of him."

"Your Honor!" Merchant yelled again.

"In my observation," Liam said, turning back to the judge. "That's what I observed." Judge Wood gave him a stern look and he blinked back innocently.

"Thank you, Liam," Kelly said. "Your witness, Counselor."

Merchant stood up and came right in front of Liam. "Liam, did you actually see evidence of this relationship? Any hand holding, kissing, anything?"

"No, I did not."

"Did Connor ever tell you, his friend, about his relationship with Jack?"

"No. I only knew of it through Jack."

"So, all you really have to offer is maybe some looks that could have been interpreted any way, and the words of a known liar, agitator, and violent animal."

"Objection, what the hell was that!?" Kelly yelled.

Merchant turned toward the audience, and I knew he was looking right at Jack. "Jack Redmond Frazier is a menace to society. He has a police record as long as my arm, starting at 11-years-old, with everything from disorderly conduct to assault and battery. He was a sociopath as a child and still is."

"That's enough!" Kelly said, leaping to his feet. "Unless you're going to put Mr. Frazier on the stand and ask him directly about his relationship with Corporal McIntyre, back off!"

The judge banged his gavel. "We're just going to pretend like none of that happened. Counselor, do you have any actual questions for the man on the witness stand and *not* the one you discarded as a witness?"

Merchant glared at Jack. I turned around and found that Jack was glaring back. So much hate between two men who had never exchanged a single word. But one thing I always loved about Jack was his sense of loyalty to his friends, to me.

"ADA Merchant?" the judge asked. "Are you done here?"

"I'm just getting started," he said to Jack, then he looked at me. I narrowed my eyes and gave him the same look Jack gave him.

Merchant finally turned back to Liam. "Thank you for your time."

I looked behind me and Jack was still fuming. Liam took the seat behind him next to Joe.

"I call Ben Jennings Junior to the stand," Kelly said, getting my attention. Barron got up and left the court-room. My forehead scrunched up in confusion. It was supposed to be Afia next.

"What!?" Merchant yelled. "His name was not on the list at all!"

"I sent a revised list to your office and the courts last night. Judge, did you receive it?"

"I did, thank you," Judge Wood confirmed.

Merchant looked at his second chair lawyer like he wanted to smack him. Barron came back into the room with BJ. Matty jumped up and stood in front of him.

"What the fuck are you doing?" he asked him quietly, but his voice carried in the cavernous room.

"Get the fuck out of my way, Matty. This has gone on long enough," his best friend said.

"You can't do this," Matty argued.

"And I need you to trust me. Your brother needs me. Your brother needs *you*. But since you're too chicken shit to stand up to *him*—" He pointed his chin at our father who was scowling at him, "—I'm going to do it."

BJ stepped around Matty and came to sit on the stand. "State your name for the record," Kelly instructed.

"Benjamin Ian Jennings the Second. I go by BJ."

"Thank you, BJ. Can you describe anything you have witnessed in the form of abuse at the hands of Staff Sergeant McIntyre?"

"I've never witnessed any physical abuse. The Staff Sergeant is clever that way. He only hit Connor in areas that could only be seen when he removed his clothing, like in the locker rooms and gyms. That's when I would see his bruises. But I knew not to speak of it."

"How did you know not to speak of it, BJ?"

"Because you just know. You just do."

"So, you suspected physical abuse. What about verbal? Emotional?"

BJ scoffed. "That was never hidden. Staff Sergeant McIntyre is a mean sonofabitch."

"Objection," the ADA said, annoyed. "Slander."

"It's not slander if it's the truth," BJ said casually.

"Objection!"

"The jury will disregard," the judge said. "Young man, this is your only warning."

"BJ," Kelly began again, "tell us about the night that Connor came out to his family."

BJ explained how he was at the bar with Sam. They both saw me lunge over the table to repeatedly punch my brother in the face. "I was going to stay up at the bar and let my brother handle it—Connor and Sam are close friends—but then I heard Connor tell the whole damn bar that he was gay, so I knew I had to get over there before something bad happened."

"And when you say 'something bad,' please elaborate."

"Meaning, Staff Sergeant McIntyre would have beat his own son in front of everyone."

"Objection! There is no way you could have known that!" Merchant yelled angrily.

"Sustained. Jury will disregard," the judge said automatically.

"I'll reframe, Your Honor," Kelly said. "Why do you think Staff Sergeant McIntyre would have attacked his own son?"

"Because I know how he feels about gay people and homosexuality. I have overheard conversations between him and my own father. They believe in con-version therapy for the women and beatings for the men. And if all else fails, the firing squad. Those are Owen's own words and my father agreed."

The ADA was furious. "Objection! Hearsay!"

"Sustained, the jury will disregard," the judge said again.

"Do you have any proof of these conversations, BJ?" my attorney asked.

"Other than hearing it for the majority of my life, no. But I do have proof of the conversation my father had with Owen that night that led Owen to go to Connor's house."

"Objection! What is this!?" Merchant was beside himself with anger.

"Overruled. What proof?" the judge asked.

BJ pulled out a folded piece of paper from his pocket as Barron handed Kelly more papers. They were phone records. Kelly passed a copy to the ADA, who snatched it out of his hand, and also to the jury. BJ handed his to the judge.

"My father called Owen from my back office at the bar," BJ said. "That's why it didn't show up on his cell phone records. They were discussing what to do about Owen's *problem*. Sam and I caught on quickly what exactly Owen's problem was. I made him get off the phone, and we got into an argument. I told him that he and Owen needed to leave Connor the fuck alone." BJ hesitated and looked at the judge. "Can I say that? I'm just saying exactly what I told him."

The judge waved nonchalantly. "Go on."

BJ continued. "I told him to leave Connor the fuck alone, that his words were striking a match on a bomb called Owen. We argued about a couple of other things, including allowing my cousin and his husband to stay with me in June. That's the last time I spoke to him."

"So, you and your father don't talk because of what happened to Connor?"

"Among other things. But yes, not in the last five months. It shouldn't have happened. The only reason the Staff Sergeant went over to that house was to make Connor come back home with his fists. Everybody knows it. You all are kidding yourselves if you think it was anything other than that. And if he wasn't coming home, someone was going to die that night. Connor did the right thing."

Merchant was done. "Objection. This is absurd testimony from a bitter son upset with his own father and trying to take out on my client."

"I'm just stating the facts here."

"No, the fact is—"

Judge Wood banged his gavel. "You will have your chance to cross examine the witness. Counselor, are you done?"

"Actually yes," Kelly said. "Your witness, ADA."

Merchant practically leaped out of his seat. "You and Matthew McIntyre are friends, correct?"

"We are."

"Do you have any firsthand knowledge of Matty's abuse?"

"I do not," he said abruptly.

"But how is it that you have firsthand knowledge of Connor's abuse and not Matty's?"

BJ shrugged. "Ask Matty. I'm not here to talk about Matty."

"But you're so adamant that Owen abused Connor. Why not Matty?"

"I'm just telling you what I saw and heard, man," he said with another shrug.

"And how do you know that these so-called bruises on Connor weren't from playing sports? Since you witnessed them in the locker room."

"Because bruises from baseball typically show up after practice, not before." He said it like was the most obvious thing.

"And how do you know that he wasn't being bullied at school?"

"Because Connor was a king in high school. Literally, they called him King Connor. Everybody looked up to him, even older kids. He defended kids who got bullied; he never did the bullying or got bullied. That's a fact."

Merchant got closer to the witness stand. "What about you? Were you abused as a child?"

"My father believed in stern discipline too, but not as much as Owen did."

"Is that why you're upset with Connor's father because he too believed in corporal punishment? Does he remind you of your own father?"

"Objection," said Kelly.

"Overruled," said the judge. "You may answer."

BJ was thoughtful. "I'm not upset with Owen. Owen reacted exactly the way anyone that knew him expected him to react. I'm upset for Connor. He's been through a lot. He finally found peace in his life. Owen had no right to try to take that away. I agree with Angie." He looked at my father. "Let him go, Staff Sergeant."

"Hey!" ADA Merchant yelled. "You don't talk to my client. You talk to me." They glared at each other. "So, your entire testimony is hearsay. You *heard* your father and Owen say this; you *think* Owen was going to do that. Is that correct?"

BJ shrugged. "Yeah, I guess so."

Merchant turned to the jury. "Right." He walked back to his seat.

"You're free to go," the judge instructed the witness.

BJ walked off the stand and nodded at me. I nodded back. He left the courtroom and Matty stormed out after him.

"Recess until tomorrow," Judge Wood announced.

I stood up and stretched, then turned to face my friends.

"Liam, Taylor, you both did great," Kelly said. "Angie, perfection. Tomorrow morning, it's Afia, then you, Jamel. In the afternoon, Connor will take the stand. Then closing arguments. I want you both back here in four hours to go over your testimony."

We all walked out together. "You're ready, Lovie?" I quietly asked Afia. "They're going to dig into everything about us."

"I know," she said confidently. "I'm ready."

"I don't want you to lie—"

"I'll do what I have to do to protect you, Connor. Like I've always done. Don't worry. It will be fine." She kissed my cheek and walked closer to her husband.

Jamel came home close to midnight after spending hours with Afia, Kelly, and Barron. I laid in the bed in the dark and waited. He looked tired when he came into the bedroom. He kissed my forehead, then went to take his shower in our en suite bathroom. After ten minutes of listening to the water run, he came back into the room and slid into the bed next to me, his skin clammy from the water.

Mel turned me onto my side without a word, and I felt the slickness of the lubricant being inserted inside of me. He slid one arm under my head as he penetrated me. I closed my eyes. He wrapped his other arm around my waist and made love to me, unhurried, as if we had all night.

I entwined my fingers with his and forgot about the outside world, the looming decision that was completely out of our hands, the stress of the day, and the anxious thoughts of what tomorrow would bring. If everything I had gone through was to lead me to that moment right there, making love with the most amazing human in the world who loved me with his whole heart, then it was worth it.

Jamel kissed the back of my neck and grazed his fingers across my nipples as he pushed in and pulled out. I moved with him, became one with him as he stroked me with his free hand. He pushed me over the edge at the same time he murmured, "Coooonooooor," and came inside me. I erupted on the bedspread and my body trembled against him. He paused but didn't pull out. I felt his breath on my neck, labored at first, then slowly coming back to normal. I rolled over, making him slide out of me, and buried my face in his chest. He held me close to him. We didn't speak for a long moment.

"Jamel."

"Yeah, baby?"

I let a moment pass. "I was going to kill him. I would have killed him for you."

He let a moment pass. "I know, Connor. I know."

CHAPTER 8

♥ • • ♥ ♥ • • ♥

Merchant Is a Dick.

Afia looked beautiful as usual in a simple blue blouse with a knee-high dark blue skirt, her hair pulled back in a ponytail. She came in with Tyrell who sat next to his brother, and when her name was called, she serenely walked to the stand. I smiled at her. She smiled back. Then as Kelly approached the stand, her face went serious.

Kelly asked about our relationship. Afia told everyone how we met on the field in her freshman year when I chased away racist bullies from hurting her. I walked her home from school that day, and we found out how much we had in common. We became inseparable. She was the only person I confided in about my relationship with Jack, and Jack was equally confiding in her. Unlike Liam, she had witnessed the affection between Jack and me.

"Connor might have been sleeping with other girls, but it was only Jack he loved," she told the jury.

She told everyone of the day she decided to become my pretend girlfriend. Someone accused me of being gay, and she kissed me in front of the whole school to dispel the rumor. "I just wanted to protect Connor for the day, maybe a couple of weeks. But Connor being attached to me meant he didn't have to be with anyone else because to the world, he was committed to me. He could ease his broken heart from his breakup with Jack without being bothered for the next couple of months until he left for the Marine Corps."

"And when Connor came home?" Kelly asked.

"Again, my decision. He was so unlike himself: sad, lost, lonely. We encouraged him to go out, meet people, Jack and I. When I realized he was exclusively seeing men, I decided to go back to being his cover story, as Jamel calls it." That made me smile.

"Why was it so important for you to pretend to be the woman on the side?" asked Kelly.

"Connor didn't want to sleep with women anymore. He wanted to explore that side of himself without his mother trying to set him up or his father asking questions. He wanted to keep other women from pursuing him. If everyone believed we were serious about each other, Connor could freely be who he wanted to be and love who he wanted to love."

"And why do you think Connor was not able to do so?"

She sighed. "I'm just going to be one more person to get on the stand and tell everyone how bad it was for Connor at home. I believe, like many others, that if his father ever found out that he was not straight, he would have tried to kill him. Which he did."

"Objection," the ADA said automatically.

"Sustained. Jury will disregard," Judge Wood said.

Kelly continued, undeterred. "When did you stop being his cover story?"

"We just gradually fell out of step with each other; the closer I got to Ty, the closer he got to Mel. We were both falling in love with other people, so we didn't need to be attached at the hip. He came out to our friends, and after that, there was no need to pretend anymore. By the time everything started to come out with his family, Ty and I were engaged, I was pregnant, and Jamel and Connor were becoming a family of two."

"What do you know of Connor and Jamel's relationship?"

"Practically everything!" she said with a laugh. "I introduced them, sort of. I gave Jamel Connor's number and encouraged Connor to give it a chance. And I'm so glad he did. Connor is so incredibly happy. The happiest I have ever seen him. They get along so well. They are perfect together. Jamel understands Connor in ways I never did, and I thought I knew everything about my best friend. And Connor loves Jamel so deeply."

"So, in your opinion, there is nothing one-sided or forced about their relationship?"

She shook her head. "Absolutely not. It is a relationship built on mutual respect. It's absurd to think that a man like Connor would be forced into doing anything he didn't want to do, especially a relationship."

Kelly ended his questioning. "Thank you for your time, Afia. Your witness, Counselor."

ADA Merchant put on his best smile as he came toward her. "Afia, you love Connor, don't you?"

"I do," she said simply.

"As more than a friend?"

"No, Connor and I are just friends."

"But there had to have been a real romantic love that you had for Connor at some point. A beautiful girl like you? A handsome boy like him? You've never had feelings for Connor?"

She answered, "Maybe at one time in my life. But not anymore. Not for a long time."

"Do you believe Connor loved you in the same way?" he asked.

She shrugged. "Maybe he did. But again, not anymore."

"If at one point in time you loved Connor and Connor loved you, why didn't you try to be in a real relationship? Why the facade?"

"Because, like I said, Connor wanted to explore other parts of his sexuality, and he would have been deeply unsatisfied with just me. And I wanted to be married with children, things that Connor did not want. Just because two people love each other doesn't mean they're compatible."

The ADA nodded and walked around. "Were you having sexual intercourse with Connor?"

I held my breath. "No," Afia said simply.

He looked at her skeptically. "No?"

"No."

"Not once in high school? All the girls he was having sex with but not you, the one closest to him? Remember, you're under oath."

"No, I did not have sex with Connor while we were in high school together. That is the truth."

"And when he came home from the Marine Corps? You weren't sleeping with Connor, then?"

Thankfully, Kelly said, "Objection, asked and answered."

"Sustained. Move on," the judge said.

Merchant paused, slipping his hands into his pockets. "If Connor wanted to be married with children, if he had decided to no longer sleep with men and be committed to you and only you, would you and Connor be together today?"

She hesitated and glanced at me. I very subtly, very slowly moved my head to the left and then to the right. She knew not to be honest. She knew to choose Ty, who was sitting in the courtroom to support her like a good husband would.

She looked back at the ADA. "No. There were many reasons that Connor and I would not have worked. Namely, his family. They never liked our relationship, and there was no way I was going to degrade myself being with someone who couldn't stand up to his own father, especially when it was obvious Owen and Matty hated me because of the color of my skin. I deserved better than to settle for that. I needed someone stronger for me, with less baggage, who was freely able to love me. I found that in Tyrell. It was easy to leave Connor behind for a better man."

I smiled. *Good girl.*

"Hmmmm…" The ADA started walking around again. "How long were you pretending to be Connor's girlfriend after he came home?"

"Four, maybe five years."

"So, while Connor was having multiple, sexual relationships with men, what were you doing?"

She didn't understand the question, but I certainly did. I scowled at him as she asked, "What do you mean?"

"I mean, as Connor was exploring sexually and using you as a cover, were you having relationships?"

"I did have some relationships, yes."

"Sexual relationships?"

"Yes."

"With multiple men?"

She finally caught on. "Excuse me?"

"Objection! Really, Counselor!?" Kelly said, disgusted.

Merchant raised his hands in surrender. "It's an honest question. If they weren't having sex together, it's a fair assumption that, while Connor was sleeping around, she needed to occupy her time with someone. Many, many someones."

I stood up in anger and Barron roughly pulled my arm to make me sit back down. "Sit down, Connor. This isn't the movies," he murmured.

The judge was over it. He banged his gavel down hard. "Sit down, Corporal. Merchant, you're on ice so thin, one move like that again, and you'll be drowning in contempt," the judge threatened while pointing his finger at him.

Merchant turned to look at me and smirked. My jaw twitched in anger. He did it on purpose, not to get to her, but to get to me. He turned back to Lovie.

"Afia, you'd do anything for Connor, wouldn't you?"

I could tell she didn't want to answer him. She was pissed at him for insinuating she was a slut. Finally, she said, "Anything within reason, yes."

"You've lied for him for many years. Why should we believe you today?"

"I lied for him to protect him from his family. I don't need to do that anymore."

"So, you expect everyone to believe you aren't going to say whatever you need to say to protect him from going to prison, after you spent so long trying to protect him from other perceived danger?"

"Only the truth will set Connor free right now. That's what I'm giving: the truth."

"Or you're trying to cover up your own part in this, setting Connor up with a controlling abuser. Maybe you're feeling guilty about that."

"Objection," my attorney called out.

"Do I really have to answer that, Your Honor?" she asked Judge Wood. "Because that is ridiculous."

"No, you do not. Counselor, be done," he told the ADA sternly.

"Sure," Merchant said smugly. "Thank you for your time, Afia."

Afia came off the stand and glanced at me briefly before heading straight to Tyrell. He hugged and kissed her, and they sat close together, holding hands, her head on his shoulder. He looked at me and I nodded at him. He nodded back.

"The defense calls Sergeant Jamel Jones."

Jamel stood up without looking at me. He wore a dark gray suit, a compliment to his eyes. After he was sworn in and gave his full name, Kelly began.

"Jamel, tell us how you met Connor."

Jamel talked about our fateful meeting at the pharmacy and everything that followed. He said, "On our first date, I asked him why no one in his family knew he was gay. He said that his family was conservative, homophobic, and racist. I asked, 'What do you think would happen if you told them?' And Connor looked me in the eye and said, 'Well my father would probably try to kill me.'"

"Objection. Hearsay," the ADA said.

"Don't worry, Counselor. Connor will tell you himself soon enough," Kelly said with a smile.

"Overruled. Continue," the judge instructed.

Jamel told the jury how close we got over the first few months. He knew to keep our relationship discreet. He described how I looked the night before I moved out of my parents' house: bruised from my face to my thighs. "It was the first time I saw bruises on his body. His father attacked him because he told him he was moving out. That's how his father reacted to his son making a decision that he didn't agree with; he punched him, choked him, kicked him. It was criminal."

Jamel talked about our relationship in general. "Connor's my best friend. We can talk to each other about anything for hours. Or not talk at all and just spend time together. He's the most loving, thoughtful, attentive man I've ever been with. And it doesn't hurt that he's easy on the eyes." Despite the seriousness of the situation, I grinned at him.

"So, your relationship is a serious one," Kelly said.

"Absolutely. He's my family now. He's a brother to my brothers, a son to my parents, and uncle to my niece and nephew. We love each other, and we're going to stay together, no matter what life throws at us, no matter how his family feels about it."

Jamel described the night when Owen came to the home, how he attacked me first, the threats, the argument, the fight, how I froze at first but then got my bearings and grabbed the gun. "Connor aimed for his shoulder, not for his head. I took my Sig from him and stood by his side. I told the Staff Sergeant if he ever steps foot in our house again neither Connor nor I would hesitate to put a bullet in his head."

"And why did you feel the need to take such an aggressive stance with him?"

"Because he would not have stopped trying to destroy his son's life. He needed to know that Connor and I meant business, as Ben Jennings said a few days ago. He didn't like our relationship, or the fact that Connor was gay, but that didn't give him the right to attack his son."

"Thank you for your testimony, Jamel." Kelly sat down and the courtroom became quiet.

Merchant sat there for a moment and stared at Jamel. Jamel stared back, not angry, not sad, not smug— just his normal, unreadable face. The ADA finally stood up and leaned on the front of his table with his hands in his pants pockets. "Sergeant, what did you know about Connor before you actually met him?"

"Nothing much. Afia told me he was a Marine Corps vet. That he had been home a few years and getting acclimated to civilian life. She told me that he was gay but only a small circle of friends knew that about him. She thought we had a few things in common and she wanted me to get to know him."

"She didn't tell you his family had strong views on homosexuality or interracial relationships?"

"No. That didn't come up until I spoke to Connor."

He nodded. "Did Connor seem like easy prey to you?"

"Objection!" Kelly yelled. "That is—"

"I can answer," Jamel interjected. "Connor is no one's prey. You would know that if you knew him, if you did your job and studied him better. He does whatever he wants to do, whenever he wants to do it. Every step of the way, I gave Connor a choice: to date, to be exclusive, to take our relationship to the next level, to move in together. And every step he took was closer to me and farther away from his father."

"And did that make you happy, pulling Connor farther and farther away from his family?"

"It made Connor happy, and that made me happy."

"Hmm…" The ADA began to pace the room. "Did you and Connor sleep together that first night?"

"No."

He raised his eyebrows. "You didn't want to have sex with the man that was easy on the eyes?"

"I wanted to get to know him better."

"Did Connor want to sleep with you that first night?" Merchant asked.

Jamel smiled at the same time I did. "He made it known that he did."

"So, you took that choice from him."

"No. I made a choice for myself."

"Hmmm… And Connor's decision to move out? Connor had been living at home for the last three years, and seven months after you came into his life, it's urgent that he move out?"

"Connor made that decision after the Staff Sergeant trespassed into his apartment when we came back from our road trip to Miami. I wanted Connor to move in with me, but again, Connor does what he wants to do. He told me 'no' and moved into his own apartment."

"Your relationship is committed and real, so you say. Do you know if Connor has had sexual intercourse with other men or women during your relationship?"

"No," said Jamel. "Connor has not slept with anyone else. Only me."

Merchant stopped pacing and faced Jamel. "How do you know that for sure? You truly believe he went from sleeping around to sleeping with just you?"

"Because I know," he said simply.

Merchant looked at him skeptically. "What kind of sex do you and Connor have?" he asked.

Wow.

Kelly must have felt the same way because he yelled, "Objection! What the hell, Counselor?"

"Merchant, where are you going with this?" the judge said tiredly.

"I can answer that," Jamel said. He cleared his throat and pulled the microphone closer, then said with a straight face and in a clear voice, "Corporal Connor Adrian McIntyre and I have *homosexual* sex. Sodomy. Fellatio. Analingus. Versatile. All ways. All positions imaginable. Some unimaginable." Then he sat back.

The courtroom was dead silent. Then, Jack snorted loudly in laughter, which set off a chuckle from everyone behind me, both of my attorneys, and some members of the jury. I went completely red as Jamel turned his face to me with the same serious expression.

I gave him a tight smile then mouthed, *I. Love. You.* He winked at me.

The judge banged his gavel twice, quieting everyone. He rubbed his forehead and sighed deeply. He turned to Jamel. "Sergeant—"

"I apologize to the court, Your Honor," Jamel said respectfully. "But he asked an absurd question which deserved an absurd answer."

The judge sighed again. "Agreed." He turned to the ADA. "Merchant, I strongly advise you to abandon this line of questioning."

Merchant was pissed. "Being the military man that you are, I assume you like things to be orderly. Controlled."

Jamel let a moment pass, then asked, "Is that a question?"

Merchant narrowed his eyes slightly. "Do you consider yourself a controlling person?"

"Controlling, no. I do have a Type-A personality and function best when there is structure around me, but I am aware that I can't control everything. And no, I don't try to."

"Being with Connor didn't help your Type-A personality, did it? His family drama didn't provide structure or order for your life."

"No, it didn't," Jamel said honestly. "But falling in love is never orderly. It's usually messy and confusing until you can get your bearings."

"But you don't like messy, isn't that right, Sergeant?"

"No. I don't like messy," he replied.

The ADA smiled. "Messy is uncomfortable. Confusion brings out the worst in someone who thrives on structure, isn't that true?"

Jamel nodded. "That is true."

"And how does one get their bearings in a messy and confusing situation, like the one you were in with Connor?"

"We had honest conversations. I told him how I felt about him, he told me how he felt about me, and we made the decision to be together. It wasn't confusing anymore because we realized it was what we both wanted."

"You never gave Connor an ultimatum? Not once?"

Jamel shook his head. "It wasn't an ultimatum. But I gave him the choice of whether he wanted to stop dating and be friends, or whether he wanted to take our relationship to the next level of intimacy."

"You mean sex."

"Yes."

"Because isn't it true that during this time you and he had yet to be intimate? That you refused to sleep with him?"

"We decided to wait, to get to know each other better, date a while."

"Did 'we' decide, or did 'you' decide for him?"

"I didn't decide for him," Jamel answered calmly but I could tell he was getting annoyed. "I told him what I was looking for. He could have decided to walk away and continue sleeping around. He didn't."

"Okay, but let's be clear," Merchant said as he stood next to the jury box. "You told Connor that you weren't going to sleep with him without a commitment, correct?"

"Essentially, yes."

"And you went to his house in the middle of the night and gave him this ultimatum—"

"Objection," said Kelly.

"I'll reframe," Merchant said before the judge could rule. "You told a man like Connor that you knew wanted to have sex with you that you could either be friends or exclusive lovers. Did you honestly believe he would have chosen anything else? Was that really a choice?"

Jamel was quiet, thinking. It got me thinking too. *Was it really a choice? If I didn't care about Jamel, would I have said yes just to sleep with him? The truth is, I probably would have. I remember saying to him that I didn't know if I was ready for a relationship, but I also didn't want what we were doing to end. Was it an ultimatum? Did I really decide on my own or did I do what Jamel wanted to get what I wanted, and it just so happened to have worked out?*

And then I remembered that Merchant was a dick and was just trying to trip up my boyfriend.

He almost had me. He almost had Jamel too; I could see him doing the same thinking that I was doing.

Finally, he spoke. "I'll repeat: Connor could have decided to walk away and continue sleeping around. He didn't. Maybe it was an ultimatum. But the difference between an ultimatum and a choice is whether you were going to lose something. Connor was never going to lose me in his life. He just needed to decide how he wanted me there, as a friend or partner."

"So, you admit it was an ultimatum. That you withheld sexual favors until Connor gave in to what you wanted."

Jamel blinked, then said, "Was that a question?"

The ADA was getting annoyed with Jamel's cool, calm, and collected demeanor. "Did you control the trajectory of your relationship with Connor? Use sex to force him into a relationship with you and tear him away from his family?"

"No," Mel said plainly.

Merchant smiled triumphantly at the jury before turning back to the stand. "Jamel, you don't like Connor's family, do you?"

"I like Katherine just fine. She's lovely," he said sincerely. "I love his sisters like they are my own. Angie and I are closer, but Mary Kate and I have developed a pretty good relationship over the last couple of months. I'd do anything for either of them."

"And what do you think of his brother Matty?"

"I don't think about his brother at all. We've never exchanged words, and I would like to keep it that way."

"And his father? You don't like Staff Sergeant McIntyre."

"No. I do not."

"Would you want to see his father dead?"

"I don't wish death on anyone. What I would want to see is for his father to stop hurting him. Physically. Mentally. Emotionally. I would want his father to let him go."

"So he could be yours? So you could keep him? Isn't that what you told his father, and I quote, 'a nigger like me already has him. I'm his daddy now. Deal with it.'"

"I did use those words, yes. After the Staff Sergeant said to me that he'd never let a nigger like me have his son. I was just using his words back at him."

"But let's be honest here: if Connor did kill him that night, you wouldn't have shed a tear."

"No, I would not have. But as upset as he was with his father, he wasn't going to kill the man that gave him life."

"Even if you wanted him dead?"

"I've already said Connor doesn't do anything that he doesn't want to do. If Connor wanted him dead, he would be. Not because of what I wanted or didn't want."

Merchant ventured closer to the witness stand. "Why did you take the gun from him, Sergeant?"

"Because it was my firearm," he said simply.

"Or because you were convinced that Connor would have killed him if you didn't?"

"I didn't say that."

"But you thought of it. Admit that, at that moment, somewhere in the back of your mind, you knew that if Connor fired another shot, it would be the kill shot."

"I was too busy trying to *breathe* after the Staff Sergeant tried to take my life to worry about what Connor was thinking at that moment."

"But you know him well enough," Merchant pressed. "You know Connor better than anyone in this room. Dare I say, better than the love of his life, Afia."

He turned around and smiled at me, then at her. Tyrell gave him an icy glare. He turned back to Jamel who was unmoved by his assertion. "What do you think Connor would have done if you didn't take the gun from him? Or even better, if you weren't there? Would Connor have killed his father?"

"I think Connor would have exercised restraint as he has done many, *many* times before when his father attacked him. He didn't kill him then. No reason to kill him now."

"And if the shoe was on the other foot? If it was Connor's neck that Owen McIntyre had wrapped his arms around, choking the life out of him? If it had been you who grabbed the gun? Would you have ended his life?"

"Without hesitation," Jamel said with a slight edge to his voice.

Merchant caught it and raised his eyebrow again. "And you expect us to believe as close as the two of you are, that Connor wasn't thinking the same?"

"The Staff Sergeant isn't my father. Connor exercised restraint because it was his father. That's the only reason he practiced restraint."

"Or maybe, you practiced restraint for him. Maybe you took the gun from his hands at the right time because Connor intended to murder his father, and you knew it. Connor took steps toward his father, you pulled him back, and took the gun from his hand and you were the one who practiced restraint that night. Isn't that what really happened?"

"I already told you what happened," Jamel said calmly. "I don't know what else you want me to say."

"Say the truth and stop trying to protect your lover, whose true love isn't you," he said in a condescending tone. Jamel gave him a slow blink, but that was his only reaction.

Kelly yelled, "Objection! Badgering."

"It's fine. He got the point. I think we all get the point." Merchant smiled at me. *I wish someone would slug him.*

"Break for recess," the judge said and banged his gavel.

Jamel came over to me and I met him in the aisle. We embraced. "That was … tough," I said into his neck. He responded by holding me tighter.

I turned and faced my friends, and they rallied around me. I addressed Afia first. "I'm so sorry, Lovie. Merchant is a dick."

She briefly let go of Tyrell's hand to hug me. "I should have expected that. That was all Matty talking. I'm either a whore or a lovesick puppy when it comes down to you."

"And we all know the truth," I said so that everyone around could hear. "You are neither of those things, just a really loyal and loving friend." She touched my face and stepped back to hold Ty's hand again.

"Who's next?" Simon asked.

"Me," I told them. "I'm the last one. I tell my story and hope for the best."

"Well, we're all here for you," Jack said.

"All of us," Benj agreed. "Don't go down without a fight, Corporal."

I smiled at him. "I promise you, I won't."

Barron tapped my shoulder. "Kelly wants you to meet him in Courtroom 536. It's empty and he wants to prep you one last time before your testimony. Alone."

"I'll be right there."

I turned back to Jamel who slid his arm around my waist. We smiled at each other, but I saw the concern in his eyes. "I'm okay," I assured him.

"I know you are, Corporal." We embraced again and I let him go to follow Barron.

TELL US ABOUT THAT.

Kelly called me to the stand. "State your full name and title."

I cleared my throat and said, "Connor Adrian McIntyre. Former U.S. Marine Corps Corporal."

"Thank you. Connor," Kelly said from his chair, "please tell us about the first time you realized you were attracted to your same-sex."

I sighed deeply. My secrets were about to come out one by one in front of my friends and family.

Here we go.

I looked directly at him and said, "When I was in the eighth grade, a beautiful seventh grade boy with jet black hair, green eyes, and dimples walked past me in the hallway, and my heart pounded. I think I knew from that moment on."

I watched Jack's eyes go completely wide. He wiped his face with his hand and used his fist to hide his smile; he was surprised, maybe embarrassed. I smiled, then cringed. "So now you know."

A small chuckle erupted from my friends. Afia and Jamel, sitting on either side of him, turned to him and smiled. I think the whole courtroom looked at him too.

"So you've always been bisexual," Kelly said.

I turned back to my attorney and answered, "I think I've always been gay. I think I became bisexual because I couldn't face what I really was. I don't think I would have started having sex with girls if I wasn't molested around that same time, at 13-years-old."

"Tell us about that."

I sighed again and confessed, "My brother Matty's girlfriend Rachel cornered me and gave me fellatio, unrequested."

"That's a fucking lie!" Matty yelled out.

I stared at him. "Is it? Really?" I know he knew what was going on. He just never did anything about it.

Judge Wood banged his gavel. "That's *never* going to happen again. You." He pointed at Matty. "If I hear so much as a whisper come from your throat again, you'll be banned from my courtroom for life."

"And you." He looked at me. "This is not an interactive circus. You direct your answers to the attorney in front of you and not to your peers. Do you understand me, Corporal?"

"Yes sir, Your Honor, sir," I replied respectfully. "I meant no disrespect to your court."

"Please continue, Connor," Kelly prompted.

"She surprised me the first time," I told everyone. "But afterward, every time Matty wasn't around she would catch me. Then, one day, she took it a step further. She came into my room and got on top of me. I let her do what she wanted, then I never let it happen again."

"I'm sorry that happened to you."

I shrugged. "It's something boys don't talk about. As a teenager, I was celebrated for losing my virginity that way. As an adult, I recognize it for what it was. Molestation. Sexual assault."

He nodded. "Tell me about growing up in the home with an abusive father."

"Objection! Leading!" the prosecutor said loudly.

Kelly rolled his eyes. "Reframe. Connor, tell us about your childhood."

"It was … hard. I had great moments. My mother is the most amazing, loving woman in the world, and I don't think I could have survived it without her. My sisters kept me sane and grounded. But despite what my brother said, Owen McIntyre was not a great father. My father believes his role is to provide for his family, discipline his children, and rule over his wife. He disciplined us with an iron fist, at least his first three children. If we stepped out of line, we were punished severely for it. Matty was rarely punished. He believed in every lie my father tried to instill in us. I did not, so I rebelled. A lot. That meant I got punished a lot."

"What kind of views did your father try to instill in you?"

I looked at the jury like Kelly had instructed me to. "White supremacy beliefs. That white is pure. That white people were genetically and intellectually superior to everyone else. That anything that wasn't white, straight, and Christian was beneath us. That people of color, especially black people, were inherently evil and nothing good ever comes from them, and that kind of evil should be rooted out and eradicated. That men were meant to rule over women and that a woman's role was to cook, clean, procreate, and open her legs for sex on demand. That liberalism was a disease that infects the world, so anyone with liberal beliefs is hellbound, and we should help bring them there. That homosexuality was not just a sin, but the worst kind of sin because it went against the very nature of humanity, the commandment to be fruitful and multiply. Gay people can't multiply so therefore they are defective and should be killed."

I watched the shock and disgust on their faces. Some looked over at Owen to see if he would show any signs to deny it. He did not. My attorney continued with me.

"Those are some pretty extreme views. When did you stop believing in your father's viewpoints?"

I turned back to my attorney. "I never really did believe in them. It was based on fear. There was just too much good in the world for everyone to be evil except us. When I started hanging out with Afia, it destroyed even the little bit I might have taken in. She shattered all stereotypes for me because, obviously, she is genetically and intellectually superior to me. She and Jack, they saved me."

"Tell us about the first time you remember being severely abused."

"I was always getting belt slashes. But when I was 7-years-old, I got into trouble for playing with my father's Korean War replicas. He backhanded me repeatedly then slammed my head against the wall. I passed out and woke up in the hospital. My parents told them I was running so fast I ran into a wall head-first. I knew to lie for them. That was my first trip to the ER."

Kelly let my words sink in for the jury. "Can you recall other times?"

"The ones that stand out?" I was thoughtful. "When I was eleven, I told my father to fuck off. I don't even remember why I said it. I think he was berating me, calling me stupid, worthless, something like that, but he made me so angry I screamed at him to fuck off. He chased me around the house, and when he caught me, he yanked my arm and threw me to the ground, bending it backward until it popped out of the socket. That was my second trip to the ER."

I tried to be nonchalant about it, but seeing the sadness, anger, and shock on the faces of my friends rattled me. But I kept going.

"When I was fourteen, he came home with a strait-jacket and told me to try it on. At first, I refused, but he put it on me anyway. After he locked it, he told me that, from that moment on, when I misbehaved, he would treat me like the animal I am. I laughed at him, and he punched me in the stomach repeatedly until I fell over. He lifted me up and put me in the corner of the room and told me not to move until he gave a shit about me again. That first time, I stayed there for three hours. He forgot about me and went to bed, so my mother took me out. My mother was usually the one to take me out. She never forgot about me."

A silent tear fell from my mother's eye, and she quickly wiped it away.

"Did you spend other times in the straitjacket?"

"Too many times. But I would rather have the straitjacket than the beatings. My father hit me at least once a week. And when he wasn't beating or berating me, he would ignore me. When I was younger, it was with the belt buckle. But after I turned twelve, he would bring me into his den in the basement and beat me with his fists. My father would punch me in the stomach and knee me in the back until I collapsed, then he would kick me in the thighs and groin until I couldn't move. I got to expect it, no matter what I did."

"Why didn't you tell anyone about the abuse?"

"Because, like BJ said, you just didn't do things like that. It was family business. And if it wasn't your family, you minded your business. I remember telling my grandmother once that I was afraid to go home. When she dropped me off, she talked to my father, told him to go easier on me. My father agreed, and as soon as she left, he took an extension cord and beat me so badly, I couldn't go to school for a week because the welts were bloody and leaking pus. They told everyone I had the flu. You talk, you get beaten more severely. So, you don't talk."

"When you discovered you were gay, you kept that a secret too?"

"Oh God yes. I had to. There was no way that anyone could know I was attracted to boys, that I was in a relationship with Jack. My father would have absolutely put a bullet in my head, I have no doubt about that. My relationship with Jack was awful because every time I felt myself getting closer, I convinced myself I was just experimenting, that I couldn't actually have feelings for a boy. I kept sleeping with girls because I needed to believe that I could switch back at any time. I owe Jack a million apologies for the way I treated him." I said the words without looking at my friend, knowing he understood, hoping he forgave me. "I'm just incredibly grateful that we're still friends."

"Well, you certainly have a lot of friends here, a lot of support," Kelly said, looking at the full benches on my side of the courtroom. He turned back. "Tell us about your time in the Marines."

"It was probably the best time in my life and the worst. I became a man overseas. I learned to care about people and things outside of myself. I became brothers with men and women of every race, color, creed, and religion. Every sexual orientation and gender. I became even more convinced that my father's views of superiority were dead wrong. Older, younger, black, white, man, woman, Christian, Muslim, Jewish: we were all the same. We all bleed red. Some were better than me, some worse, and my genetics or masculinity had nothing to do with it. But we also lost a lot of good men and women. I almost lost my own life a few times. It was my brothers that kept me sane. Those amazing men right there. And Vinnie."

I pointed to Taylor, Simon, Joe, and Benjin. All four raised their arms and saluted me. I saluted right back.

"Since Taylor brought it up, I'm going to ask you about the relationship you had with a private. What can you tell us?" Kelly asked.

I swallowed. "I'm just going to call him B. B was like me, from a conservative family and in the closet. We fell in love and kept our relationship quiet, for obvious reasons. It was my first adult relationship. Since we were in the same position, it didn't have the same angst of someone wanting me to come out. We had secret codes and messages with each other. We met in secret. It was hidden and freeing at the same time. We had to hide, but I was able to love him freely, and he was able to love me freely too. It was all we had…" I had to stop talking, I was getting emotional.

Kelly noticed and went to the table, pouring a glass of water. He handed it to me. I drank it all in one gulp as everyone waited. "Do you want to talk about how it ended?" he asked gently.

I thought it through. If they thought my lover was still alive, they may not compel me to say his name. But if they knew he was dead, then they might, saying that it did not matter. So instead, I said, "It just did. We said our goodbyes and it ended."

Kelly nodded, understanding. "Let's switch gears. Why did you leave the Marines?"

I inhaled and exhaled. "When Vinnie died, it affected all of us. I was the Corporal of my unit, but Vinnie was the glue that held us together. Once he died, we became unglued. Joe and I watched Vinnie die and it affected him tremendously. He left first. Benjin and Vinnie were also close, so he lost his desire for the mission and left. I too lost sight of why I joined in the first place. I was no good to anyone emotionally, so I came home. Taylor and Simon left because I did."

"Tell me about your first year back. How was it being back home again, with your father?"

"For once, my father treated me with respect. But that didn't last long. A week after I came home, I went for an early morning jog with Jack. When I came back, my father got in my face about hanging out with a known gay man and called him names. A month after that, I brought Afia over for Sunday dinner, and the next morning, he punched me awake and choked me because Matty told him we were sleeping together. My father told me that if I got her pregnant and had a mixed-race baby, he would kill me."

He actually said he would kill her and whatever nigger babies we had, but I left that out. Afia never needed to know that.

"So because he already believed the lie that you and Afia were together, you decided to let him and everyone else continue to believe it?"

"Yes. It was just easier since the set up was already there. And I wasn't ever going to get her pregnant because I wasn't sleeping with her. If I was out with a guy, I would just say I was with Afia and they wouldn't question it."

"Connor, I'm going to ask you some personal questions, okay?"

I was ready for them. "Yes."

"When you came home from the military, were you sleeping with any women?"

"No, I was not sleeping with any women."

"So you were exclusively dating men."

"Dating is a stretch. But yes, I was exclusively with men."

"So, you were having sexual relations with men, years before you met Jamel?"

"Yes."

"How many men do you think you have been with?"

I sighed. "If I had to ballpark it? Probably upward of sixty to seventy men in a three-year period. Maybe eighty. And that's just the ones I had actual intercourse with. I had sexual encounters with over a hundred and fifty men. Maybe two hundred."

I saw a couple of mouths drop, including my mother's, Mary Kate's and Angie's. The rest either knew or didn't care. I ignored Matty, Stephanie, and my father's looks of disgust. I was thankful that Jamel didn't flinch.

"Why do you think you had sexual relations with so many men?" Kelly asked me.

I shrugged. "Partly making up for lost time. I hadn't had the opportunity to really explore my sexuality before then. It became addicting and I became insatiable. I loved sex and it was something I was good at. Great at. I loved the thrill of keeping this secret, how many times I could get away with it and nobody would ever know. I was hiding, but I was free to be me.

"But also, self-hatred. It was that part of myself that I kept hidden because I thought everyone would hate it. I didn't know who I was, didn't know my own self worth, didn't respect my mind or my body. I thought I was just protecting my heart. I had only two male partners before that, both I loved and lost, so it couldn't be a good thing that I was attracted to men. I didn't want to be emotional about another man, I just wanted to—excuse my language—fuck and forget. I didn't want a relationship, I just wanted to explore, and then, I don't know, find a woman to settle down with. Maybe Afia if she wasn't married with kids by the time I was ready. Live a mediocre life." I didn't look at her as I spoke.

"So what changed for you?"

"Mel. Sergeant Jamel Josiah Jones. He walked into my life when I was nowhere near considering a relationship. I absolutely just wanted to sleep with him and move onto the next. But he…" I smiled to myself. "He made me feel something that I've never felt before. Safe. Whole. Valued. Like I finally had someone who fully understood who I was. Jamel did give me a choice to be friends or to be committed partners. Call it an ultimatum if you want to. But I'm so thankful that we didn't just sleep together and go our separate ways. He's literally the best thing that has ever happened to me. He changed my life, changed me for the better."

"Tell us about your relationship."

"Oh, man." I smiled again and looked at the jury as Kelly had instructed. I told them how I stopped smoking, stopped drinking heavily, stopped sleeping around, and committed all of my time and attention to him. How he encouraged me to take my organization to the next level and supported my dreams. How he loves me.

"Mel and I are like peanut butter and jelly. We just mesh so well. We have so much fun together. We like the same things. We have the same beliefs and values. He just gets me, you know? I don't have to say a whole lot. He knows what I need when I need it. He loves me fiercely. And my love for him is like no other. Jamel is the love of my life. But yeah, he's my best friend too."

Kelly asked, "Is your relationship mutual?"

"Absolutely. The Major, Jamel's father, told me once that his only concern was how two alpha males were going to make it work. But we do. It's give and take. It's compromise. It's how well we communicate and relate to each other. We don't argue. I know that sounds crazy, but if we have a disagreement, we talk it out. Jamel taught me that. I know I'm a pain in the ass. I know I get emotional and needy. But Jamel is so emotionally mature, solid, a steady rock in my life. We're good together. He's my perfect match."

Kelly changed gears again. "How did it feel to come clean to your friends and then members of your family?"

I smiled at everyone who smiled back at me. "Jack, Afia, Winter, and Mina have always known. Liam too, apparently—I just found that out yesterday. When I told my other friends, they were so supportive, so welcoming of Jamel in my life. My friends are the best."

"And your family?"

"I wish I would have told my sister Angie years ago. That was one of the first things Jamel told me. He said, 'Tell Angie. Something tells me she would be okay with it.' And he was right because when I did tell her, she immediately embraced me, embraced Jamel, and became part of the circle of people who knew the real me. Mary Kate found out when I confessed to my family at Angie's birthday party. She too surprised me with how readily she accepted Jamel in my life. My sisters and his brothers hang out all of the time now. It feels good to have the people that know you and love you know your truth."

"How does your mother feel about it?"

Without looking at her I said, "I know my mother loves me unconditionally. Before the incident, we had a talk and she understood why I made the decisions I made. Why I chose to hide from them. She knows who my father is. But how she feels about everything now? I don't know because my father is keeping her from me. I haven't spoken to my mother in months."

Kelly stood up and went next to the jury, so I was facing them again. "Tell us about the incident, what happened that night when your father came to the house."

I repeated the same things I told the detectives. "I grabbed the gun and aimed for his shoulder. I fired one shot and it connected with my target. He let go of Jamel's neck and I pulled Jamel closer to me. I told him all the things I've been wanting to tell him since I was child: how awful of a father, husband, Christian, man in general that he was. I said the words, 'I should kill you,' but I did not fire the gun again. It was not my intent to kill him. Scare him? Yes. See the fear in his eyes that he has seen in my eyes for 28 years? Without a doubt. Let him know I was dead serious about him leaving me alone for good? Absolutely. But kill him? No."

"What happened next?"

"Jamel took the gun from my hand and pulled me back to him. He pointed the gun at my father and told him to get out and never come back, or we would invoke Stand Your Ground. My father left, holding his bleeding shoulder. We sat down and ate in silence. Angie banged on my door, and I told her what happened. She left to go find out where he went. Then I took pictures of Jamel's face and neck, just in case. We assumed my father would send the police after him for the fight. But instead, my father sent the police after me."

"And what has your life been like since the incident?"

"Good in some ways. I'm free for real now. I don't have any fear of being found out because everyone knows who I am and who I love, including the one I feared the most. But awful too because this has torn my family apart. Angie being kicked out of the house just because she accepted me—that's not fair. Mary Kate is in shambles; she's not eating or sleeping, crying all the time, worried about me, worried about my father, worried about my mother. And I'm worried sick for my mother. I'm so afraid that he's hurting her because of me. I'm grateful that at least Mary Kate is still in the house. Someone has to watch out for my mother."

"And you? How are you doing?"

I looked at Jamel. "I'm afraid. I'm afraid that every-thing that I've been building for myself was shattered the moment I picked up Jamel's gun. I'm not afraid of facing the consequences of my actions. I'm afraid of being separated from him. I think it would kill me."

I watched Jamel take a deep breath and exhale slowly through his nose, his face softening. It took me a moment to realize that Kelly was done with me, and Merchant was calling my name.

"Connor?" I turned to the ADA. "Are you a liar, Connor?"

I resisted the urge to roll my eyes. "Everybody lies at one time or another. But no, I'm not a patho-logical liar."

"But you lied to everyone. For years. Decades. You lied about your sexuality, your promiscuity, your rela-tionships. Why should anyone believe anything you just said on the stand if you are known to be a liar?"

"Objection," Kelly said curtly.

"Sustained," the judge decreed. "Feel like starting your actual questions, ADA?"

Merchant glared at him but then said politely, "Yes, Your Honor." He turned back to me. "Connor, do you love your father?"

"Yes."

"Do you believe your father loves you?"

"No."

He was surprised. "No?"

I shook my head. "No. Angie is a lot more optimistic than I am regarding my father's love. He loves his daughters, he loves his first-born son, and he tolerates me. There's something about me he has always disliked, and it showed in how he has treated me my whole life."

Merchant looked at me curiously and asked, "How did he treat you differently? Because it sounds like you all were disciplined sternly, were you not?"

"Yes, for the most part. It was just in the way that he treated me."

"So, if your father thought you were in danger, he wouldn't come to your rescue?"

"I'm sure he would. He would do his duty to me as a father would a son. That doesn't mean he cares about me."

"But how were you treated differently, Connor? Did he give your siblings hugs and tell them that he loved them and not you?"

"No, my father doesn't do that."

"Were you fed the scraps while everyone else ate well?"

"No. My father never withheld food from us. Even if we were punished, we were always fed."

"Did he have heart to heart conversations with Matty, or Mary Kate, or Angie, and not you?"

"No. He doesn't do that."

"Were you the only one that received his biblical lectures or his monologues of white superiority?"

"No, we all did."

"So how was he different with you than with everyone else?"

I hesitated. "It's … hard to explain. It's a feeling I've always had."

"So, you went through life believing that your father had some kind of disregard for you because of how you *felt?*"

I became a bit flustered. "He was harder on me than the others. He just was. Maybe because he saw something different in me. I don't know."

He smiled at me. "Did you think you were special, Connor? Did you need to be coddled and doted on at all times? Hugged and told everything was going to be alright, that the world was going to love you regardless of who you became? Did you need participation trophies and gold stickers so that you knew you were loved?"

I didn't answer him. He was being a condescending dick and he knew it.

"Connor, if it was Matty that he heard was being seized by a gentleman, how would your father have reacted?"

"Objection," Kelly said. "'Seized?' Really?"

"It's what his father believed, Your Honor."

The judge sighed. "Sustained. Continue. Carefully."

"I'll reframe. Connor, if it was Matty that had taken up with a gentleman, something he had never been known to do in his entire life, do you think your father would have reacted differently?"

I thought about it. "No. He would have reacted the same way; he would have tried to force him back home."

"So, again, why do you think that you somehow got worse treatment from your father? That he was somehow only a mean sonofabitch to you?"

"I don't think he was only mean to me. I know he treated us all with the same visceral behavior. I just happened to get it more because I didn't toe the line."

"Exactly and—"

"But that doesn't make it right!" I talked loudly over him. "It wasn't right what he did to Mary Kate that night and then what he did to Matty. I thought my brother died. I thought I was next. You don't know that type of fear, Merchant. You don't know what it means to grow up in a house with a psychopath, who legally owns twelve firearms, who felt he had every right to beat on you no matter how old you were, just because he gave you life. You don't know what it feels like to start taking blows or have a gun put to your head and think to yourself, 'Is this the day he kills me?' You're asking me if my father loved me? I don't give a shit if he loved me or not. He didn't come to my house out of love. He came to my house because having a gay son embarrasses him, ruins the McIntyre reputation of having a pure and good Catholic family. So, if that's his love, I don't want it." I looked directly at my father and said, "Owen McIntyre can go to hell."

I heard my voice echo in the silence of the courtroom and felt rage burning in my chest. Owen's jaw twitched in anger as he glared at me. I glared back.

Merchant came closer. "Are you angry with your father?"

"Yes."

"Angry enough to want to kill him?"

"Objection!" My lawyer yelled.

"Overruled, the witness will answer," the judge said.

I turned away from Owen. I took a moment so I could control the edge in my voice. "If you would have asked me that ten years ago, even five years ago, I would have said yes. I hated him because he hated me, and that was before he knew I was gay. But now, I'm more sad for him than angry. He's lived his whole life in fear of others, fear of diversity. What a sad and pathetic life."

"You didn't answer the question," he said nastily.

I kept calm. "No, Merchant. Not angry enough to want to kill him. Not anymore."

He stepped back and smiled at the jury as if he just won something. "When Owen and Jamel started fighting right in front of you and you froze, where did you go, mentally?"

I looked up at the ceiling before I responded, "I had a flashback."

"Flashback of what?"

"Of a time that I almost died in Iraq."

"Tell us about that."

"I'd rather not."

"Your Honor," he complained to the judge.

Judge Wood said, "Corporal, please answer the question. What you remember."

I looked at him and nodded. "Vinnie, Taylor, Joe, and I were trapped under heavy fire in an abandoned house. We didn't think we were going to live. Joe was repeating 'There's no way out' and Taylor was screaming at me to get us out of there."

"And what were you doing in the flashback?"

I glanced at Taylor, and we locked eyes. I knew he remembered that day just as vividly as I did. "I was … thinking about the people I love. People I may never see again."

"So, you retreated back to a time you felt helpless."

"Yes."

"And, in real time, you were feeling helpless again, unable to help the people that put their trust in you, like Jamel."

"I suppose so."

"How did the situation resolve itself in Iraq?"

"Another unit came from behind and took out the insurgency for us."

Both of Merchant's eyebrows went up. "So, you failed."

"What?" My forehead scrunched up.

"You. *Failed*," Merchant said forcefully. "You failed to protect your men. Someone had to come and do the job for you. That's your testimony, isn't it? That you failed to keep your men safe, and as a result, they almost died because of you?"

I glanced at Taylor, Simon, Joe, and Benjin again. They were all scowling. Their anger made me smile. I turned back to the asshole in front of me.

"You sound like someone who has never served a day in their life," I said coolly and sat back, clasping my hands in my lap.

He threw his hands up. "I'm just acknowledging your failures. You failed then, and you almost failed again, nearly allowing your father to kill your partner. The partner that you hid behind, thinking he was going to protect you. But he didn't. He failed too. Two failures living under one roof. How sad and pathetic."

"Objection, badgering," Kelly said from his seat.

"Sustained." The judge glared at the prosecutor.

I, on the other hand, smirked as he continued. "Is that why you grabbed the gun, Connor? Because you didn't want to fail again?"

I shrugged. "Maybe. Maybe I was tired of feeling helpless. Maybe I was tired of being afraid of him."

"But you failed again because you didn't kill him."

I shrugged again, shaking my head. "Wasn't my intention to."

Then Merchant came all the way up to the stand and said in my face, but loud enough for everyone to hear, "I bet if it was *Lovie* you would have killed him dead."

That wiped the smirk off my face.

How dare he use the name Lovie? He's lucky my hands are in my lap. He's lucky we're in a courtroom and not on the streets of Providence or the Iraqi desert.

"Objection!" Kelly yelled.

Merchant stepped back with a smile. "No further questions."

Kelly stood up. "The defense rests."

"Okay," the judge said. "It's been a long day, so we'll recess until tomorrow morning and do closing arguments. Then the jury will adjourn."

I sat there a moment longer as everyone else rose. I watched Ty leave the courtroom with Afia, and she never glanced back at me. Then I got out of the seat and went to Jamel.

"You're good?" he asked.

I nodded. But I was mentally exhausted, like I had gone ten rounds with Mike Tyson. But no TKO happened. He didn't win. I survived. Jamel touched my face affectionately and I leaned my cheek into his palm.

My unit came over to me. "You never failed us, Corporal," Benjin said first. "Not then, not now."

"Yeah, fuck that bitch," Simon said, glaring at the ADA. "Somebody should toss him in Fallujah and see how he makes it out alive, then let's see him talk about failures, fucking dickhead."

I patted his shoulder and gave him a reassuring smile. "It's all good, Sy. Let's just go. Dinner at my house."

As we walked out together, Jack fell into step beside me. "Middle school? Really?" he asked quietly.

I cringed, then smiled at my best friend. "Now you know."

"Jesus, Connor." Jack shook his head and smiled back.

CHAPTER 10

HONESTY, ACCEPTANCE AND FORGIVENESS

Merchant's closing argument was more of the same: I hate my father, I wanted to kill him, blah blah blah. Surprisingly, Kelly handed off the closing argument to Barron, and he did well. He was poised, calm, and succinctly laid out the facts for self-defense. He kept using the phrase, "By the letter of the law." And by the letter of the law, I acted in self-defense. We were done by 11:30am.

And all we could do was wait.

We waited in the courthouse all afternoon, but by 4pm Kelly said, "It's a good thing they didn't come back right away. That means they are actually deliberating, weighing the options. That there is reasonable doubt in some of the jurors. This is good. I suspect I'll get a call from Merchant soon."

We went home and waited, not sleeping all night. The next day, we went to the courthouse again, stayed all day, and nothing. We went home again. Day three, we did the same, coming to court and waited. Jamel and I went out for lunch, ate in silence, and came back to the room. But this time, Merchant was sitting in a chair next to Kelly, looking as happy as ever.

"Corporal," he said with a smile. "Good to see you and the Sergeant in such good spirits." I blinked at him.

"Get to it, Alex," Kelly demanded. "What are you offering?"

He stood up. "Second degree aggravated assault. Three to five."

"Fuck off," I said viscerally.

But Kelly held his hand up. "You can do better than that. The jury didn't come back right away. It's either a hung jury or an acquittal. We both know this. Do better."

He sighed and waved his hand nonchalantly. "Simple assault. One year."

"Eat shit," I responded.

"Connor—" Kelly started but Merchant came over to me with his hands in his pockets.

"You're facing ten to twenty years, Corporal. Now I know a community of cocks is a dream come true for you, but prison won't be what you think it is. Think of how much you'll miss Lovie," he said sarcastically.

"Merchant, you're crossing the line here!" Kelly boomed.

I stepped closer to him, my face to his, putting my hands in my pocket to stop myself from putting my hands around his neck. "Just say you want me to fuck you, Alex. Say you want me to bend you over this table, slide my nine-inch dick in your ass, and make you feel pain and pleasure. It's what you've been dreaming about since the moment you laid eyes on me. It will make you feel a whole lot better." I licked my lips and smirked at him.

He smirked back. "You haven't been paying attention. It's me fucking you, Corporal. Fucking pretty boys like you is what I do. It keeps my nine *and half inches* hard." He stepped back. "Get your client to take the deal, Kelly," he said as he walked out. "He won't get anything better."

As soon as he closed the door I stopped smiling and punched the wall. "FUCK!" I screamed, pressing my forehead against the ruined plaster. Jamel touched my shoulders, putting his body against mine. We stood that way in silence.

Kelly spoke softly, "What do you want to do?"

"I don't know," I murmured. "I don't know."

"Lirion, I'm taking Connor home. We're not coming back here," Jamel decided without me. "We'll consider the offer, but if we don't take it, we'll wait at home."

"Okay," Kelly agreed. "Keep your phone on at all times, day and night."

Jamel took my hand without another word and led me out of the courthouse. When we got to my car, he put his hand out. "Give me the keys." He started the car and began to drive, letting me stew in silence.

I couldn't believe my life had come to this. Every time I thought I'd dug myself out and was finally free, something happened to destroy all my hopes and dreams. Facing the real possibility of sitting in prison, whether for one year or twenty, was breaking me down. I finally understood what Owen did by coming after me. He wanted to separate me from everyone, not just Jamel. From my mother and my sisters. From my friends and everyone that had accepted me. Owen's abuse was never just physical. It was psychological. And, once again, he had me right where he wanted me: at his mercy, feeling like there was no way out. I hated Owen for this. *No matter what happens, I will never forgive him.*

Hot tears sprang from my eyes before I could stop them, and I choked back a sob. Jamel immediately pulled over, put the car in park, and pulled me into his arms. He held me and let me cry, something I had not done since I cried on Jack's shoulder when this whole thing started.

Jamel didn't try to comfort me or tell me it would be alright because he didn't know if it would be. And neither did I. He held me close until I calmed down. I sat up and wordlessly moved away from him, and Jamel drove us home. We didn't talk. I just went upstairs to lay down while he made dinner. I weighed my options. I considered taking the deal. It was still a felony charge and having a felony would limit me considerably, but at least I would be out in a few months with good behavior. I could continue to do what I had been doing with my organization. But I hated the idea of giving in and letting Owen and Merchant win. I debated gambling with my freedom with the jurors. If I won, I would get to go home and put this nightmare behind me. If it was a hung jury, that asshole Merchant was sure to bring me back to court again and the nightmare would continue. If I lost, I would go to prison and the nightmare would never end.

Jamel knocked on the door. "Dinner's ready. Come downstairs."

I did as he asked and couldn't help but to smile. My loving boyfriend had dimmed the lights, lit candles, and made a picnic in the living room. He laid out a blanket with bowls of spaghetti covered with homemade sauce and meatballs, fresh garlic bread, and salad. A glass of Riesling was already waiting for me. I sat down across from him on the blanket and made my bowl. We quietly ate and it was filling and comforting. My dogs came around and ate scraps, and Diesel put his head on my legs, like he just knew I needed the comfort. Afterward, I laid down and stared at the ceiling. Jamel came closer and put his head beside mine, laying the opposite way on his stomach. He gave me an upside down kiss, then he put his head down.

We laid in silence for a while. "What do I do?" I whispered.

He was quiet for a long time, then said, "I think you've already decided what you're going to do."

"Yeah? What did I decide?"

"You're not going to take the deal. You aren't going down without a fight. If they're going to try to take you down, then you're going down swinging. You're not going to give Merchant or Owen the satisfaction."

I smiled without looking at him. *He thinks he knows me so well.*

"Call Kelly and tell him to tell Alex to eat shit and die. Make sure he tells his client too."

❤

Two days later, we got the call from Barron. "Jury is back. Meet us at the courthouse in one hour."

Jamel turned to me. "Who do you want me to call?"

"No one. Either I come home, or I don't." He nodded, but then I changed my mind. "Tell your folks and my sisters. That's it. Just family."

"Okay."

We drove over without talking. They were already waiting for me at the top of the steps: Major Wendel Jones, Mama Denita, Lavell, Donny and Ty, with Afia, Angie, but also Jack. "Who told you?" I asked Jack.

"I called him," Lovie said. "He's family, too."

"And you know I'm always here for you, Connor," he said sincerely. "You'll never go through this alone." I gave him a small smile and patted his shoulder.

We all walked into the courthouse and the courtroom together. Everyone looked at my entourage. Mary Kate smiled at me, and I smiled back. Owen scowled at me but also at all the faces around me. He truly hated the fact that I was loved.

When everyone was seated, I turned to Jamel, but I couldn't speak. He slowly ran his hand through the side of my hair, across my neck and shoulder, down my arm, and held onto my wrist. We stared at each other, then I gently touched his face and put my forehead on his. I closed my eyes and allowed myself to feel all my feelings for him. No words were needed between us. *He knows I love him, and I know he loves me, now, forever, and always. If I go away, he'll wait for me.*

I stepped back first and gave him a chaste kiss on his lips before sitting at the defendant's table. I would not turn back around no matter what the verdict was.

"You're doing alright?" Kelly asked.

I nodded. "But what do you think?"

"In my experience, it's smelling like a hung jury. And if it is, we may need to prepare again. If it's a guilty verdict, we'll appeal right away and do this again. Either way, we'll still be fighting. You're ready for that?"

I nodded. "Whatever it is, I'm ready."

I sat there with my St. Christopher pendant in my hand and flipped it seventeen times, reciting a Hail Mary with each flip. My rosary hung on my rearview mirror, but I kept St. Christopher with me every single day of my life. I'd never had to take it out and use it, but I did then. I needed all the help I could get.

Finally, the bailiff called, "All rise, Judge Gabriel Wood presiding."

We stood until the judge came in and sat down, then he said, "The jury may enter."

I watched the bailiff open the side door and the jurors filed in. Some glanced at me, but most did not. No one smiled. I had no idea what to expect.

The judge turned to them as my heart pounded out of my chest. "Madam Forewoman, please stand." Juror Number One stood up. "Have you come to a verdict?"

She sighed. "We have not. But—"

I exhaled, realizing that I had been holding my breath. The audience murmured. "I knew it," Kelly said quietly.

The judge banged his gavel. "Please continue."

She began again. "We the jury are unable to come to a consensus on the charges laid forth by the prosecution. After five days, we are irrevocably deadlocked.

We have penned a statement that we would like to read to the court with the permission of Your Honor."

"Proceed."

She unfolded the paper in her hands and began to read. "In the matter of The People of The State of Rhode Island and Providence Plantations versus Former Marine Corp Corporal Connor Adrian McIntyre, we the jury are unable to come to a mutual verdict on the matter set forth before the court. Here are the circumstances: Nine members of the jury find the defendant, Corporal Connor McIntyre, not guilty on all accounts. Two members of the jury find Corporal Connor McIntyre guilty on the charge of attempted manslaughter. One member of the jury finds Corporal Connor McIntyre guilty on the charge of attempted murder.

"To the prosecution: the Assistant District Attorney failed to fully make the case of attempted murder by the letter of the law, leaving an abundance of room for reasonable doubt in the majority of the jurors' minds. If the matter is to be taken to court again, the evidence of Corporal Connor McIntyre's intent of homicide, even in the throes of passion, must be sound and grounded, which at this time, it is not.

"To the defendant: three members of the jury were convinced of the intent to further harm the senior McIntyre based on decades of inflicted physical, verbal, mental, and emotional abuse on his son Corporal McIntyre. And while we all personally believe that the intent was warranted, by applying the letter of the law, the three jury members believe that had Sergeant Jamel Jones not stepped in at the right moment to ensure his partner did not inflict further harm, the senior McIntyre would have lost his life on the night in question.

"All twelve jurors and four surrogate jurors believe that self-defense was not strongly taken into consideration. The plaintiff entered the defendant's home aggressively, so the intent to harm his son was apparent; the matter should have been resolved outside of this hearing. Pertaining to the matter of the charges before us, this resulted in a split decision on how to apply the letter of the law. While we understand that a hung jury decision provides an opportunity for the State to bring charges again to Corporal McIntyre, we unitedly and strongly advise this matter not be taken to court in the future. The prosecution does not have a full case. And this family, especially Corporal Connor McIntyre, has been through enough. Thank you."

Stunned, I sat in silence. Then I crossed myself and breathed out, "Thank you, God."

The judge sighed too. He looked at Merchant, who was pissed. He looked over at me and I tried not to look too happy. At least for today, I was going home.

"Corporal Connor McIntyre, please stand."

I did, and Kelly and Barron stood with me. "The jury was unable to come to a decision in regard to your guilt or innocence. For now, you are free to go. But I caution you to get therapy and talk to a professional about everything you have been through. It is evident you have a lot of anger toward your father and your brother. Maybe even your mother. You obviously have a lot of love and support around you, but if you don't deal with your internal issues, it will begin to affect the positive relationships you have created. Your relationship with your father is forever changed, but you have the power to keep the relationship with your mother, your brother, and sisters civil as you go on with your life."

Then he turned to the prosecution. "Staff Sergeant McIntyre, please stand." My father stood up and straightened out his suit jacket as I had done. "Staff Sergeant, I along with many others in this court, have been horrified to learn of how you have raised and abused your children, physically, mentally, and emotionally. You've inflicted harm that will continue to haunt each member of your family, maybe for generations. Look at your daughter behind you, who has cried every single day of this trial. Look at your wife, who has been holding it together, but she is broken. Look at them, Staff Sergeant!"

My father's jaw twitched in anger, but he did. He turned around to look at Mary Kate's tears, then at my mother who was, at first, stone-faced but then put her head down. "Look at the hate you've instilled in your eldest son; you've literally turned brother against brother. Are you proud of yourself, Staff Sergeant?"

Owen turned back to the judge but didn't answer. "Your Honor, this is highly—" the ADA started.

"Shut up, Merchant!" he yelled at the lawyer. "All you've done is brought circumstantial evidence at best, and at its worst, poured gasoline on a family whose house was already burning. I agree wholeheartedly with the jury: you'd better not end up in my court, or any court, with this case again unless you have some actual evidence to present."

The judge leaned back, visibly upset. "Staff Sergeant, if you actually do care about your family, you will find a way to make amends. Allow your wife to see her son. Allow your daughter to move back into your home if that's what she wants to do. And if your amends at this time is to never speak to your son Connor again, to finally let your son live his life so that he may begin to heal from the pain you have done to him all these years, then that, sir, is the least you can do.

"If I could order intense, weekly family therapy for the entire McIntyre family, trust me, I would. You all need healing, even you, Staff Sergeant. And it starts with honesty, acceptance, and forgiveness."

He turned to the jurors. "I thank you for your service. This hearing is concluded in a mistrial due to a hung jury. The defendant is free to go." The judge banged his gavel for the last time.

I stood there for a moment in disbelief at the words, "free to go." I heard the hooting behind me, and I knew my friends were celebrating. But I was taking in the judge's words. *Maybe I do need therapy because I definitely still have some deep-seated issues which need to be addressed. Owen is dead to me, but I still need to at least try to repair the relationship with my brother, without anger and animosity, and continue to let my sisters make up their own mind about a relationship with Owen.*

Kelly pulled me out of my thoughts by animatedly shaking my hand. "Nine jury members were willing to acquit. Merchant would be a fool to try this again." We both looked over at him, talking with my father and brother, all three scowling. "I will talk directly with the district attorney to ensure he drops this. So go home, Connor. It's over."

"Thank you," I told him. "I literally owe you my life."

"Just keep doing what you're doing out there for vets, Corporal," Kelly told me. "Pay it forward and we're good, for life."

Silently, Barron packed up the desk. "Hey," I called to him.

He looked at me and smiled. "Congratulations, Connor."

"You did an amazing job for your first real trial case." I touched his arm. "You're a fantastic attorney, Barron."

He shrugged. "It wasn't an acquittal."

"But they heard you. Your closing argument was phenomenal, and they heard you. It's because of you that I'm not on my way to prison right now. Take the win. Because I'm forever grateful to you, too." He smiled and we shook hands.

Finally, I turned around to face them, my family. Nine smiling faces all holding each other, waiting for me. I walked over to them and Angie and Lovie got to me first, both hugging me tightly. Then Mama Denita and Jack. My brothers-in-law hugged me too. And lastly, the Major surprised me by giving me an awkward hug.

Jamel was the only one that did not hug me. Instead, he took my jaw in his hand and kissed me square on the lips, making me blush. He took my hand in his and said, "Let's go home, baby."

We walked out together. My mother and father were nowhere to be seen, but Mary Kate was waiting for me on the sidewalk. I left the Jones family and walked over to her. She practically ran into my arms. I picked her up and spun her around.

"I'm so happy for you! I love you, Connor! I love you so so much!" she cried.

"I love you too, Mini Kat."

"I promise I didn't choose them over you. I—"

"You don't have to explain, MK. You owe me no explanation, just as long as I know you still love me after what I did to our family."

"Oh Connor," she said as I put her down. "You didn't do anything to our family. Dad did. He did all of this to us. He'll make amends. I'll make sure of it."

"You don't have to—"

But I was cut off by my brother shouting, "Hey! You!"

We both turned our heads to watch Matty bravely approach the entire Jones clan with Stephanie right behind him but even more stupidly get in Jamel's face.

Matty said, "You said you never exchanged words with me. Well, exchange words with me now, bitch."

Jamel kept calm and said, "Get you stupid ass out of my face, Matty."

"Make me," Matty snarled. "Everything that happened is your fault. You should have left my brother alone. You destroyed our family. You're gonna pay for all of this."

I started walking over. But before Jamel could respond, Ty pushed him back and stood in his way. "We haven't officially met yet. I'm Tyrell."

"Ty. No." Afia grabbed his arm, but he forcefully pulled out of her grasp.

Matty smirked. "Oh, so you're the one that got second place, after my brother wore that nigger pussy out—"

But his statement never fully came out because Ty punched Matty in the mouth, then wrapped both of his hands around my brother's neck, pinning him against the wall. A scuffle ensued, with Donny, Lavell, and Mel trying to pry their brother's hands from around my brother's throat and me in the middle trying to pull them apart. Once they managed to remove Ty's fingers, I pushed Matty back against the wall. He coughed up blood and phlegm, then threw up.

But Ty wasn't done. He spit right in Matty's face, barely missing me. "That's for my wife and daughter, you racist piece of shit!" he screamed at Matty as his brothers pulled him away. He continued to scream and curse Matty out from down the block while Jack, Afia, and Mama Denita tried to calm him down.

I turned toward my asshole brother. "Matty, what the fuck!? Did you not hear a word the judge said? Are you not even trying to bring this family back together?"

"Fuck that judge! And fuck you! The damage is already done!" he yelled back at me, wiping Tyrell's saliva off his cheek. "I only stayed around to give you a message: Give him back everything he's ever given you, like the car. Don't ever step foot in his house again. You wanted your freedom from him? You got it. He will never have anything to do with you again. You're no longer his son."

"What!?" MK exclaimed.

"He can't be serious," Angie said right behind her.

But I held my hand up to stop them both. "Owen stopped being my father the day I put a bullet in him. Tell Owen from the bottom of my heart to go to hell. I have a father now."

I stepped backward and turned my back on my brother. *So much for acceptance and forgiveness.*

The Major was still standing there. He watched the whole thing and did not intervene in any of it. I just stared at him, knowing he heard me acknowledge him as my father.

"Let's go, son," he simply said. "You ladies are welcome to come too."

Angie and Mary Kate looked at each other. "I'm going with Connor," Angie said.

MK nodded. "I'm going to the house to talk to Mom and Dad. I'll call you." They embraced and then went in opposite directions, Angie following me and MK walking behind Matty and Stephanie.

 # CHAPTER 11

NOTHING WILL EVER
BE THE SAME.

I had no idea where the Jones brothers went. Angie and I went in the car with The Major and went to their home. It was quiet. We were the first to arrive. The Major went to his bar and poured three glasses of bourbon, handing a glass to Angie and me. He lifted his in a toast. We followed suit.

"To freedom," he said.

"To freedom," we both repeated. I smiled and took a sip.

"Let me know when they get here," he said. "I have some things to take care of in my office, then I'll join you." He left us in the living room. I took off my shoes and slumped into the closest chair.

Angie sat next to me. "I can't believe it's finally over, at least for now."

"Kelly said he's going to the D.A. to make sure Merchant doesn't bring it back to court again."

"That's great!" she said happily.

"Yeah, it is."

I wanted to be happy, but I wasn't. *This whole thing brought out some deep-seated issues, huge cracks in my family, maybe with some of my friends too. Nothing will ever be the same.*

Angie must have sensed my melancholy. "Connor, it's going to be alright," she said softly. "Things are going to be different for the McIntyres, but maybe for the better." She was quiet for a moment then said, "I'm not moving back in."

I sat up. "You have to, Ang. You have to make sure Mom is okay."

"I can't, Connor. Dad and I… Everything I knew about my father has changed. I knew he could be mean and cruel, but after everything that I learned? Our relationship is forever changed too. He'll always be my father. But I won't ever look at him the same."

"Mom," I reminded her. *Fuck Owen. Who's going to protect my mother?*

She touched my hand. "I know you're worried about her. But she told me that she isn't going to allow us to babysit her. She doesn't want me to move back home. She said I was free now, and she wasn't going to allow me to get sucked back in."

"Ugh," I groaned. "She's going to kick Mary Kate out too, isn't she? She's trying to set us all free from him."

"I think so. Mary Kate's job is taking her closer to Boston anyway. Or she may move in with me and help me with the rent, so you and Jamel don't have to pay for me anymore. She may have other plans. I don't know. We haven't talked about it yet."

I shook my head. "I don't like this at all."

"I don't either, really. But what can we do? She's never going to leave him. She made that clear to me."

"Me too," I said, remembering when she told me that her place was right by his side.

We heard the front door open. Mama Denita, Donny, Lavell, and Afia came upstairs, looking exhausted. "I'll go cook dinner. Afia, want to help me in the kitchen?" their mother asked.

"Yes, ma'am, just give me a second to call my mother to bring the baby over." Afia sat on the other side of me.

"Where's Ty, Jack, and Jamel?" I asked, sipping my bourbon. Warmth settled in my belly.

She shrugged. "They went for a drive in your car."

I looked at my best friend. "Are you okay, Lovie?"

She sighed in annoyance. "Oh, Connor. I fucking hate your brother." I smiled and Angie giggled. "I'm sorry Angie, I really, really am, but *ugh*. Between the trial and what he just said, it's bringing up all these past issues that I thought Ty and I had resolved. But it's triggering him."

"But nothing was happening between the two of you, right?" Angie asked. "So, he has nothing to worry about. I mean, I was fooled, and so was everyone else; It just seemed so real between you two."

We stared at her blankly. Then I turned back to Afia. "I'll talk to him, Lovie. I'll remind him that we've always been just friends. That it's him that you love."

"Thanks, Connor. I'm going to call my mom now." She got up and left the room.

Angie grabbed my bicep. "Connor? Nothing happened between you and Afia, right? You didn't lie on the stand … right?"

I looked her in the eyes. "Let it go, Angie. Afia and I aren't together and never really were. And that's all you need to know."

Lavell came into the room before she could object. "Hey Ang, you have…" He glanced at me then back at her. "A phone call."

Her head looked up at him expectantly. My face scrunched up. "Phone call? From who?"

But Angie jumped up and grabbed the cell phone from his hand. "Thanks, Lavell." She took the phone and went toward the back porch.

He turned to walk away but I asked again, "Lavell, a phone call from who?"

He smiled and said, "Ask her. I'm staying out of it." He followed her out.

"Guess I'm not the only one keeping secrets," I said out loud, alone in the living room.

The house was full and Mama Denita and Afia cooked like it was Thanksgiving dinner: platters of baked chicken, ham, baked ziti, mac and cheese, fresh rolls, yellow rice, cheesy broccoli, and garden salad covered the table. Dr. Adina brought Tykeya over, and Mel and Ty came back an hour after everyone else. Jack came over with Ethan and their two children, 6-year-old EJ and 9-month-old Jackie, and he told me that Mina and Winter were on their way too. Mary

Kate showed up last, right as the food was hitting the table. We pulled chairs from every corner of the house and flooded the dining room. Major Wendel said grace and we dug in. The room was lively with good conversation, love, and laughter.

Between bites, I marveled at how well everyone was getting along. Just two years ago, I was still hiding who I was from most of the people around me. Last year, I was still hiding from my family. And here I was, surrounded by so many people that knew and accepted me. My heart was so full of love and appreciation.

As dinner wound down, I stood up. Everyone immediately quieted. I held up my glass. "I just want to thank you all for standing by me all these years. Afia and Jack, I survived my childhood because of the two of you. I discovered what love and acceptance looks like because of the two of you. All the good parts of me are because of the two of you. Thank you for always being there for me.

"Winter and Mina, the two women who accepted all of me from the moment they found out and gave me the courage to be myself. You were the first people in my life to do so outside of Jack and Afia. Ethan too. Just being there gave me the courage to stand up to my father that day. Your friendship is invaluable."

I turned to my sisters and touched my heart. "You have no idea what it means to me to have my baby sisters, my flesh and blood, here with me, supporting me, standing with me. Still loving me. I love you two so much it hurts. No matter what happens with our family, I will always be your big brother and will never turn my back on you because you never turned your back on me." They held hands and smiled at me, tears in their eyes. I held back tears of my own and turned to my brothers.

"Ty, Donny, Lavell, I've never known brotherly love until I met the three of you. Thank you for adding me to the Jones line up. You have me, always.

"Major Jones, Mama Denita, from the moment I met the two of you, I wished you were my parents. And now you are, and nothing has made me happier that you've embraced me as a son and a member of the family. Thank you so much for your unconditional love and support of Jamel and me. And although my mother is not physically here, she is here in my heart, and we'll be together soon. I know it."

I turned to him. "Jamel." I paused as he looked up at me with those grey eyes of his that still take my breath away. We stared at each other as I rubbed his head. "Every single moment with you makes me happier than the one before. You have my entire heart. It's you and me, for life." I leaned down and kissed his lips in front of everyone and took his hand in mine.

I turned back to the room. "I love you all. I don't know what the future holds, but I know for a fact that every single person in this room will be a part of it. Thank you for standing by me."

Mama Denita spoke for everyone. "We love you too, Connor, all of us. Your siblings. Your friends. Your partner. Me and the Major. We all truly do." There were nods and smiles all around.

Mary Kate caught me on her way out. "So, Dad wasn't kidding. He wants the car back. And he's cutting you out of his will. I'm sorry, Connor."

I shook my head. "I meant what I said, Mary Kate. He's not my father anymore. He wants the car; he can have it. I don't want his money or anything to do with him." I changed the subject. "Are you moving in with Angie?"

"I'm thinking about it. I just feel like I'm 24-years-old and still living at home, and I need to branch out on my own."

I smiled. "Branching out to live with your little sister?"

"Shut up," she said with a shove. "Plus, I might have … someone really special in my life."

"Ah, the plot thickens," I teased.

"Shut up!" She shoved me again.

Angie came over just then. "Did she tell you the good news?"

"Yup, she did. And I can't wait to meet him."

"Meet who?" She looked at me, alarmed.

I looked at Mary Kate. "So, you have someone in your life. And you," I pointed at Angie, "have someone in your life too, and both of you are hiding them from me." They looked at each other, then looked away. "Uh-huh. I know I've been a little occupied with this whole going to prison thing, but now that that's over with, why don't you introduce me to them and I'll figure out whose skull to bust open first, yeah?"

"Ugh, I have to go," Mary Kate said abruptly, walking away.

"Yeah, me too," Angie said, following her.

Jamel and I took a shower together that night. When we came out, he sat on the end of the bed and I stood between his legs, holding my cock. I rubbed it against his pretty brown lips and he opened wide for me. I moaned and held onto his shoulders, gently thrusting as he sucked me. I pulled out slowly from his slick mouth.

"Lay down," I ordered. He did without another word, and I put my tongue in his mouth, trying to devour him.

I kissed along his neck, down to his pecs and abs. I kept going until my lips wrapped around his cock. I slowly but firmly blew him, making him grunt over and over. When he was nice and hard, my mouth traveled farther down, greeting each testicle with a kiss and a suck until I made my way to his aching hole. I tongue kissed his anus as aggressively as I tongue kissed his mouth minutes ago, digging my entire tongue past the ring, licking around inside and out, up and down, making him squirm. Just the thought of how close I came to not being able to do this again had me wanting to taste every inch of him.

Eventually, I moved back up to kiss him again, my tongue tasting like him. Jamel grabbed my hair tightly and pulled me close. He must have been feeling it too, how close we came to being apart. He held onto me as our cocks moved against each other, and we loved each other with our mouths. I came up for air first, leaning over to grab the lube off the nightstand. He stayed still, keeping his knees up and his eyes on me as I inserted the gel inside of him. I knelt before him, stroked myself a few times, then gently entered him. He groaned and grimaced but let me in. I began to move. I closed my eyes and disappeared into his unbelievably tight and moist tunnel, once again losing myself in him. I felt him reach out and pinch my sensitive nipples, making my already electrified body shiver. I surprised myself with how long I held him in that position, but soon I needed to pull back before I came too quickly.

I pulled out and said, "Turn around."

He did, arching his back. I slid back inside of him and moved with urgency, one hand on his waist and the other on his shoulder. I felt him move with me, our moaning in sync. I'm a proud shit-talker during sex, but I didn't that time. I could only concentrate on pleasing him.

He reached below and began to stroke himself so I knew he was close. I angled myself to graze against his prostate and he let out a whimper. I loved that whimper; it meant I was hitting it just right. Over and over and over again, I pounded that sweet ass that I got to call home until he said my name, "Coooonoooor," and I felt his entire insides squeeze me as he released onto the bed.

"Fuck, baby, FUCK!" was all I could get out before my eyes rolled back and I dumped a ton of cum inside of him. I slowly pulled out, but I wasn't done. I kissed down his spine and licked the crack of his ass, pulling his cheeks apart to lap up my cum. He laughed at the sensation of cum trickling out of him as I licked his thighs.

"You're so fucking nasty," Jamel teased me.

I moved up to his mouth with his cum still on my tongue and kissed him. He grunted and grabbed my face. He turned around and I straddled him. He kissed me back just as aggressively as when we started.

I pulled back and said, "And you get to love my nasty ass for the rest of your life."

He smiled at me. "That sounds like a marriage proposal."

Um what!? My eyes widened and he laughed hysterically. "You can eat the cum out of my ass, but marriage is going too far!?"

I laughed with him. "What can I say? I'm an enigma."

Jamel pulled me back to his lips and kissed mine softly. "I get to love your nasty ass for the rest of my life."

I put my arms around his neck and held on. *For the rest of my life.*

❤

Jamel's phone buzzed us both awake in the middle of the night. He looked at it puzzled, then answered, "What's wrong?"

I heard Ty's voice. "Open the door, Jamel. I need to talk to you. Just you."

Jamel looked at me and I gave him the same confused face right back. "Okay. I'm coming down," he said into the phone.

He hung up and began to put on a pair of sweatpants and a long-sleeved t-shirt. "Something with Afia?" I asked.

"I don't know yet," he said. "Stay here." He kissed my lips and went downstairs.

I stayed in bed and heard the door open. They spoke quietly, then I heard the French doors to the backyard open. I tossed and turned for a few minutes, then I decided to just text her.

[Connor: What's wrong with Ty?]

[Lovie: Where is he?]

[Connor: Here. Talking to Jamel.]

Lovie did not respond. I waited another two full minutes, then texted again.

[Connor: ??? Lovie???]

[Lovie: I told him everything about me and you.]

Shit!

I looked at the words, closed my eyes, and exhaled. I knew I shouldn't be upset, but I couldn't help it. If she didn't tell him years ago when they first got together, I didn't understand why she had to tell him now, especially after all these assertions of us being in love. Ty and I just got to a place where we were cordial to each other and this was sure to ruin it. I tried to call her, but she cut the call short sending me to voicemail. She texted instead.

[Lovie: I can't talk. Not to you. Not right now.]

Which meant she was crying and scared that he was going to leave her over this. That her feelings were all over the place and talking to me would just confuse her more. I sent one last text to reassure her:

[Connor: Okay. I'll handle it. It will be okay. I love you.]

Even though I wasn't sure it would be. And she did not text me back, not even to say I love you too. That was a first.

I put on a pair of sweatpants and a tank top. Even though it was cold, I found them downstairs on the back porch.

I heard Ty say, "...be so nonchalant about this."

"Because it doesn't matter," Jamel said. "It was five, six years ago. Three years before you even met her. You can't hold it against her."

"I don't. Except that she should have told me."

"But you were already insecure about their friendship, Tyrell. If she would have told you back then, you know what you would have done. You would have cut and run."

"I wouldn't—"

"You would," Jamel cut him off. "And you would have missed out on all you and Afia have, all because you let your insecurities get in the way. Don't let it get in the way now."

"You're missing what I'm saying, Mel. I'm not insecure. I'm a realist. Connor is... He's gonna cheat on you one day. You and I both know it. And I don't want it to be with Afia. The moment y'all break up, he's going to try to take her from me."

"I'm not worried about that at all," Jamel said. "And neither should you."

"Ty," I spoke up. "That's never gonna happen."

They both turned to look at me, then Ty turned back to Jamel and gave him an exasperated look. I kept talking. "It was a long time ago, and we've maintained our friendship, nothing else. Afia loves you. Afia is in love with you, not me. You are her happiness. What we did, what we had... That doesn't even come close to what you have with her."

He scoffed. "Because what you have with her is eternal love in every other universe but this one?"

Fuck, she really did tell him everything.

I swallowed. "Because her love for *you* is eternal, deeper and stronger than anything she has ever felt for me. She didn't lie on the stand. You are the better man for her. You've always been. You're her one true love, not me."

Ty walked over to me aggressively and stood in my face angrily. I stayed calm, but I didn't back down. "I know I'm a better man, Connor," he practically snarled. "I am a million times the better man. Not just for Afia. I'm a better man than you, period. And I don't trust you."

He glared at me until Jamel said his name quietly. "Tyrell. Go home to your wife, Ty."

Tyrell backed up slowly, hate etched all in his face. He silently walked out of our home. I put my hands on my head in despair and spun around to face Jamel. He closed the back door, then leaned against it, watching me.

"Are you upset with me that I didn't tell you?" I asked.

"Not upset." He shook his head. "It's not like I didn't know. You and Afia are way too close to have never slept together. I just don't understand why you didn't tell me yourself. You were adamant that you didn't sleep with her as adults. You made it sound like it was like a one-time experiment in high school. Not during your time in the Marines. And not after. And not this whole idea of being together again one day."

I came closer to him. "Because we didn't tell anyone, not even our friends. I wasn't trying to keep things from you or lie to you. I was just trying to protect her. She didn't want anyone to know."

"Okay," he said. "So, do you want to tell me now, now that Ty knows? Because I'd still rather hear it from you, from your perspective."

I sighed. "Lovie and I are just friends. We've never had a real relationship. We've been close friends longer than anything else." I paused and he waited. "I got a pass to come home from the Marines to take her to prom. She asked me to take her virginity that night. So, I did." He nodded slowly but didn't speak. "We slept together one more time when I was vulnerable about losing Vinnie, and we both needed to feel something. Then we decided not to do it again unless we were going to be serious about each other. And we never did it again because we never became serious about each other."

"Because you didn't want to be?" he asked. "Or because you just assumed she would always be there for when you were ready? To live a not-so-mediocre life with her." I opened my mouth, then closed it. He nodded slowly again. "That right there is what Ty is worried about. That somewhere, in the back of your mind, you think that if things don't work out, you will try to get her back."

"That's not gonna happen," I said right away. "Because I would never do that to them, to her. I'm not that fucking selfish! And because *we* are not going to ever be over." Jamel said nothing, just blinked at me. That made my heart drop in my stomach. "Are you worried about that?"

"No," he said simply.

"But...?" He didn't speak, just looked at me. I turned around and hit my fist into my palm. "Fuck, Mel!" I grumbled through gritted teeth. I paced the length of the living room.

"Connor—"

"No!" I turned back and yelled at him. "You said... you told me that you were not threatened by my love for her!"

"I'm not," he said quietly.

"Then what the fuck!" I yelled back. "Now you don't trust me too?"

"I didn't say that."

"You're not saying anything! I just wish that, for once, you would just yell and scream and tell me what the fuck you're thinking!" I screamed at him.

"Would that make you feel better?" he asked calmly. "If I yelled and screamed at you?"

"It would make me feel better if you believed that I wouldn't leave you one day for Afia!"

"Connor, I don't think that. I think you're misunderstanding how I feel."

"Then what then!?"

Mel sighed. "Sit down." He motioned toward the dining room chair.

"No, I'll stand, thanks." I glared at him.

He came closer. "I trust you, Con. But I need you to trust me too. I want you to trust me with all the parts of you. Even the parts you think I won't be able to handle. I can handle honesty. I just need you to be honest with me, always."

"And I have been," I told him. "I told you what I feel for you is stronger and deeper than anything I've ever felt before. Even for Afia. Even for Vinnie."

"And I believe you."

"But?"

"I just want you to believe it too."

"What does that *mean?*" I whined.

"It means…" He touched my shoulders. "That you have to know that I'm in this for the long haul. I'm not worried about things not working out between us. They already are working out. But any doubt in your mind will lead you to fall back on your safety nets, your old habits when things get rough between us, because they will. We have an amazing life, and we'll weather some storms, like we did with the trial. But through it all, you have to know that I'm your safety net, that I'm not going anywhere."

"I know that, Mel. Afia is not my safety net. She was—I'm going to be honest. And you were right when you told me in the beginning of our relationship that I was holding onto this idea of us to keep myself from being attached to anyone else. From finding what I want, need, and deserve. But I always said to myself, if she was married and happy, I would let her go. I let her go a long time ago, mostly because she was happy, but also because I was happy too."

He nodded. "Good. But know that Ty is going to struggle with this, probably for a very long time. Maybe forever. And you are going to have to be sensitive to that. Your relationship with him was always rocky, but it might get rockier for a while. So, no more digs at the idea of her being your girl around him or even how close you two are. He's not going to take kindly to that. If a situation arises, you're going to have to be the adult in the room. You back down first. Can you do that?"

I sighed. "Yeah. I can do that."

"Okay." Mel pulled me close and kissed me. "And before you ask, no, I'm never going to leave you, Connor. Not over this or anything. Never."

I closed my eyes and put my head on his shoulder.

♥ • • ♥ **CHAPTER 12** ♥ • ♥

SLOPPY

I sat at the bar at Red Rock after work and drank. I hadn't spoken to Lovie in three days, and I missed my best friend. I kept getting harassing texts from Matty to return the car, which I had paid for outright. I still hadn't heard from my mother. The trial was over. But the nightmare continued.

I was hurting. I was pissed. And all I wanted to do was drink.

"Last one, Connor. You're getting shitfaced," Sam said as he passed me another tequila-infused drink with a curse for a name.

"Just give me the Motherfucker, motherfucker," I slurred.

Sam shook his head. "Just park the car in front of the house with the keys inside and get another one. It's not that serious. Let him have it." I had been complaining to him all day about the car, but not about Afia. That pain I kept close to my heart.

"But it's my car, Sam. My fucking car. Do you remember how excited I was when I got it?"

Sam smiled. "I do. We drove all through Providence screaming out of the windows."

I smiled too. "Yeah, that was so fun." I took a gulp. "It's not fair. He tried to take everything from me and when that didn't work, now he wants to be petty."

Sam began again, "So just give him—"

"That's not the fucking point!" I yelled loudly, getting everyone's attention. "It's MY CAR." I drank another gulp and sulked.

"So then keep the car," a voice behind me said.

I turned around and there was Jack. I grinned at him, and he grinned back. He put his arm around my shoulders. "You don't have to give it back. Just tell him to fuck off. He can't repossess it from you because it's in your name and paid for. So, keep the car."

"That's what Mel said," I mumbled. "Just ignore him and keep the car. But the other part of me feels like … I don't want it anymore. Because it's the last thing he ever did for me. So, he can have the fucking car. I wish I could shove it up his ass."

Sam scoffed. "Connor, make up your mind, my dude. You're just going in circles now." He grabbed a few takeout bags and handed them to Jack. "It's all paid up."

"Thanks," Jack said as he grabbed them. "Hey, come back to the Inn with me. We're just having dinner. Nobody feels like cooking tonight."

"Yeah, get him outta here," said Sam. "And his car stays here in the lot. He's not driving anywhere."

"I wasn't gonna. I promised Mel. I was gonna call a cab, honest," I told them both.

"Well, come to the house and sober up, then I'll take you home," Jack decided.

I grinned at him. "You're always there for me, Jack."

"And I always will be," he said automatically, like he typically did. "Let's go."

I slid off the bar stool and waited until things stopped spinning before I followed him. Sam ran up and put my coat on me before I stepped out the door. Christmas was in a few days and the air was frosty. Jamel was working on a house in Massachusetts with his father, and I knew I wouldn't see him for another couple of hours. Jack and I walked in silence, leaving me in my thoughts.

I missed her so much. If I knew letting her go would hurt this much, I would have never let her go. But I didn't call her, and she didn't call me. So I guess Ty finally got what he wanted: for our friendship to be over. I also missed my mom, a lot. But I hadn't called her either because I was afraid to get her in trouble.

I lost the two most important women in my life and it's all Owen's fault. If it wasn't for that stupid trial, none of this would have come out. But then I thought about it again.

"No, it's my fault," I said out loud, remembering I was the one that picked up the gun.

"What's your fault?" Jack asked.

I shrugged and didn't speak for a moment again. "Afia and I aren't friends anymore." He didn't respond. *Of course Afia told him. They're friends too.* "How much do you know?"

"She called me. We talked." He let a moment pass, then said, "You're still friends, Connor. She loves you.

She just needs to put her husband first. Give her some time."

"Her husband hates me," I murmured.

"Can you blame him?" Jack responded. "Carlos talked that same shit to Ethan, that they were always going to be together in the end. Carlos believed that shit too. But when I came along, everything changed, and he couldn't handle it. So he tried to come between us."

"I would never try to come between them," I implored.

"But Ty doesn't know that. All he knows is that he needs to protect what's his. Just like I did with E. Once he understood that I wasn't fucking around with him, he backed all the way off."

"But you still hate Carlos. And their friendship is not the same as it was when they were kids," I reminded him.

"I do still hate Carlos," he admitted. "And no, they don't talk as often anymore. It's better this way."

"How is this supposed to make me feel better, Jack?" I whined.

He turned to me in the street. "It's not. It's supposed to make you stop feeling sorry for yourself and being selfish. She has a family. She loves you, but she has a husband that she has to put first. And so do you, by the way. Your lives have changed considerably. Give her time, give her space, and back off. Let her figure out how to keep you in her life and still honor her husband."

"And if she can't?" I said sadly.

Jack put a hand on my shoulder. "She can. You won't lose her. It will be different. But you won't lose her."

I nodded. We walked into the Inn together. As soon as I entered the basement apartment, EJ's face lit up.

"Uncle Connor!" he yelled and ran up for a hug.

I gave him a big one. "I can't believe you're about to be 7-years-old, little bud."

He grinned at me. "Yup, I'll be seven and then eight after that," he told me proudly.

Ethan came over and gave me a brotherly hug, then said, "You smell like the bar."

"Yeah, I'll take him home after he's had some sustenance in him," Jack said as he dropped the bags on the table.

EJ followed me to the living room talking non-stop, distracting me completely from my troubles. I sat down and JC crawled her way to me, gesturing to be picked up. I chuckled and put her in my lap. She settled herself completely and leaned into my chest. I looked back and saw Ethan and Jack whispering as they set the table and prepared plates; I knew it was about me. I didn't care. I listened to EJ's stories and felt the warmth of a baby on my chest, and it made me feel better. Moments like that made me think that I might be happy with having kids of my own with Mel. *Something tells me he would be happy to have them with me too.*

But then I remembered that *I'm a fucked up individual with an abusive childhood, a whoring past, and an obvious drinking problem, so no, I won't be ruining a child's life with a shitty upbringing and emotional issues.*

"Let's eat," Ethan called out.

I looked down and JC had fallen asleep on me. I carefully stood up and walked over. Jack tried to take her from me, but I told him, "It's okay. She is sleeping on my left arm; I can eat with my right."

I gently sat down, cradling the baby. They all held hands, with Jack's hand on my left shoulder. Ethan said a quick grace and we dug into our pepper steak and rice pilaf, courtesy of the Red Rock Bar and Grill. I watched their family dynamic and I wondered how they did it. Jack had major trauma in his past, but he was the best father. Ethan too; I didn't know his whole story, but I knew there was promiscuity, drugs, and alcohol involved. But somehow, they found each other, clung to their relationship despite the issues, and created a beautiful family. I realized what the difference was. They both had fathers that loved them, accepted them, and stood by them. I didn't have a father growing up. I had a warden.

"I'm going to drive him home in his car and take a cab back. You're okay tonight with the kids?" Jack asked his husband.

"Sure, we'll be fine," Ethan replied. "Hurry back." They kissed each other and Ethan gently took Jackie from me. "Bathtime, kid," he told EJ.

EJ hugged me first. "Can I have a sleepover at your house with Freddie?"

I sighed, not knowing if it would ever happen. "I'll let you know, okay, EJ?"

"Okay," he said happily, practically bouncing down the hall.

Jack turned to Ethan to talk and I glanced at the bar near the kitchen wall. I walked over and took a bottle of Jack Daniels that was halfway done. They both turned to look at me. "For the road," I said with a smile, twisting off the cap.

I stepped out into the night air and took a swig. I hadn't been that drunk in a while, and I knew Jamel wouldn't be happy seeing me like that. I took out my phone and turned it off, just in case he called. I just needed to be sloppy for the night, without his disappointment. I started walking back to Red Rock, drinking along the way.

Jack caught up to me and we walked in silence back toward the bar to pick up my car. He took the keys from me and went to the driver's side. But he didn't start it. Instead, he watched me drink from the bottle.

"Do you know how lucky you are, Jack?" I asked.

He rolled his eyes. "Connor—"

"I mean, yeah, I know, your parents were murdered. Obviously, that's not … lucky." I took a swig. "But then you got a whole new set of parents that accepted you and loved you every single day of your life. And then this guy just dropped into our town and just … fell in love with your crazy ass. He and his son. I mean, that kid…" I took another drink. "EJ loves you, Jack. And Ethan's father, I bet he loves you too. And his mother. You've always had adult role models that just … love you."

I tried to take another drink, but Jack snatched the bottle out of my hand. "Are you done with the pity party?"

"I don't have a father," I said sadly.

Jack took a sip from the bottle. "You do have a father. His name is Wendel Jones. And from the moment you met him, he's taken you in like a wounded animal and nursed you back to health. Wrapped his arms around you. Protected you. Given you wisdom, love, and support. So, stop this shit. You don't need Owen to love you anymore. You don't need his approval or acceptance. You have a dad who does all that now."

I sighed. "Take the car back, Jack. Just park it in front of the dealership with the keys in there after you drop me off."

He turned on the ignition. "Why don't we do that now? Get some closure. Then we'll walk back to my car, and I'll take you home."

He didn't wait for a response before he began driving west. When we got there, we saw the gate was open. It was supposed to be locked, but every once in a while, one of Owen's employees screws up.

"Someone is going to get chewed out tomorrow," I said as Jack drove right in. The silver sign, McIntyre Motors, gleamed as my headlight strafed across it. "Park it right in front of the window."

I stared at the car's reflection in the glass before I got out of the car, grabbing my rosary off the rearview mirror and putting it around my neck. Jack followed me to the trunk as I pulled out a garbage bag and began to empty out the items from there into the bag. Jack emptied out the glove compartment and the side pockets. I was almost done with the trunk when I heard him yell, "Arrrgh!"

"What?"

"Why the fuck do you have a dildo under your seat!?"

I smiled with the trunk door still up. "You really wanna know?"

"I am not touching that shit!" he yelled, his voice echoing in the darkness.

I slammed the trunk down and came around to the side of the car. I bent down and picked it up. "It's actually a bobble-head thing. An old lover gave it to me years ago."

"Oh," he said, relieved. I handed it to him. "So it's not a real dildo?"

"Of course it is, you just suction it to the dashboard."

"Arrrgh!" He yelled again and dropped it. I busted out laughing and he shoved me. "Asshole," he growled.

I bent down into the car and grabbed the bottle, then threw the keys on the driver's seat. I sat on the hood of the car. Jack sat next to me. I drank and passed it to him, and he drank and passed it back to me. "Don't forget you still have to take me home," I reminded him.

Jack held his hand out for the bottle. "It's no fun getting wasted by yourself. You'll stay at the Inn, and I'll take you home in the morning."

I nodded and handed him the bottle. We drank and laid on the front of the car for a long time, the cold no longer an issue because of the alcohol in our systems. "I forgive you, you know," he said, breaking the silence. "For being a shitty boyfriend in high school. I wish I would have known everything you were going through back then. I wouldn't have pushed so hard for you to come out. Just know that I forgive you for anything you said or did when we were kids, trying to figure ourselves out."

"I barely forgive myself for being a shitty boyfriend to you," I mumbled.

"I know that," he said. "I heard you on the stand. But it wasn't awful. We weren't awful together. Toxic as fuck, but we also had a lot of fun. We experienced a lot of things together for the first time, and I am glad it was with you. I have no regrets about us being together, so let that be one less thing on your conscience."

I was quiet, then asked the question I probably shouldn't have. "Do you think we would have made it? If it wasn't for my father? Would you and I be together right now?"

He took some time to answer. "I don't know, Con. If you had the chance, would you want to change anything about us? Our lives, our partners? Would I have been better for you than Jamel? Would you be better for me than Ethan?"

"Honestly? No. Does that hurt you?"

Jack scoffed out a laugh. "No, it doesn't. Because I feel the same way. I wouldn't change a thing about us in high school or our friendship now."

"Same." I held my hand up and he grasped it tightly. We laid there holding hands, something he always wanted to do and I never did. It didn't feel sexual, but it did feel affectionate. It made me think of Afia again.

"I miss her," I said quietly.

"It's okay to miss her. Just give her time."

"Okay." I was thoughtful again. "I hate him."

"That's okay too."

"He's dead to me. Owen McIntyre is dead to me."

"Just Owen?" he asked.

"Yeah. I'm not cutting Matty off because of Freddie. I love that kid like he was my own. And he needs EJ in his life." Jack didn't respond but I heard him sigh.

"I won't let Owen come between me and the other members of my family. I'm getting my mom back somehow. I'm keeping Freddie in my life. Fuck Owen. He tried to take everything from me, and he lost. I'm fighting to get it all back. That's the biggest fuck you I could ever give him."

Jack squeezed my hand. "Fuck him. That homophobic, racist, sonofabitch. Someone should ram that dildo right up his ass," Jack said with a laugh.

And then I got the idea. "Get up."

"Huh?"

I sat up and hopped off the car. "He wants his car back? He's gonna get it."

Jack sat up and watched me grab the dildo off the ground and slide into the driver's seat. "Connor, what are you doing?"

I started the car and suctioned the dildo to the dashboard. The uncut cockhead bobbled around a little.

Jack jumped off the hood and opened the passenger side door. "What are you doing, Connor?" he asked again.

"I'm ramming this dildo right up his ass," I said with a smile.

"Connor—"

"Get in and put your seatbelt on or close the door," I told him seriously.

"Connor!"

"You got five seconds ... four ... three ... two ..."

Jack jumped into the car and put his seatbelt on. I smiled at my best friend, who was just as crazy as I am. "You ready?"

"I got a family, Connor. And so do you," he reminded me. "We have a lot to live for."

"Don't worry. I'm not gonna kill us," I assured him. "The airbags will make sure of that."

He looked at me with alarm. "Connor!" he yelled, but I had already put the car in reverse and back up about twenty feet.

Jack grabbed onto the door handle and said very fast, "Hail Mary Full of Grace the Lord is with thee blessed art thou among women and blessed is the fruit of thy womb Jesus Holy Mary Mother of God pray for us sinners now and at the hour of death Glory be to the Father and to the Son and to the Holy Spirit. Amen." He crossed himself.

I don't know why I found it so funny, but I started giggling, then stomped on the pedal. The car screeched and flew straight for the window. It was like an out of body experience. I glanced over at Jack whose eyes were bugging out of his head. To his credit, he didn't scream. I turned back just as we crashed through the glass.

I pressed the brake immediately and we skidded to a halt on the showroom floor, bumping two desks out of the way. Shockingly, the car window cracked but did not break, and the airbags did not deploy. We looked at each other then turned to see the entire 20-foot glass window had shattered into a million pieces. The security alarm blared angrily. We turned at each other again and laughed, then jumped out of the car, leaving the key in the ignition and the dildo bobbing on the dashboard.

We hauled ass, running over shards of glass and jumping through the window frame. I grabbed the garbage bag of stuff off the ground as we sprinted past. We didn't stop until we were about two miles from the dealership, then doubled over on the nearest park bench. We were both hot and sweaty, despite it being around seventeen degrees outside.

When I was able to catch my breath I said, "Holy fucking shit that was awesome."

Jack started laughing. "Fuck, we ran in the opposite direction. Afia's parents' house is a block away." We both started laughing again. "C'mon. Let's go home."

We walked back to the Inn talking, reminiscing, laughing, play-fighting. When we made it back, it was dark so we walked in quietly. But the main dining room light was on, and Ethan immediately appeared, with Mel right behind him.

"Where the fuck have you two been for over two hours?" he asked angrily. "You didn't answer your phone!"

"Whoa. Calm down, *Dad*," I joked. Jack snorted in laughter.

I found out later that when Jack didn't return within the hour, Ethan called Jack's phone, only to find out that he had left it on the counter. He called my phone, and it went straight to voicemail. He called Mel, and Mel said I had never arrived. Mel drove around looking for my car, worried about me. He had been there for about thirty minutes before we showed up, looking like we didn't have a care in the world.

Ethan looked like he wanted to punch me in the face. "Connor—"

Jamel touched his shoulder to calm him down. "Let's go, Con. Give me your keys." He held out his hand.

Jack snorted again, making me laugh. I put both my hands in the air and said with a grin, "Poof! They're gone!"

Jack laughed out loud and fell against the wall. "Oh shit, oh shit!" he cried between laughter.

The puzzled irritation on both Ethan and Jamel's faces was enough to keep us laughing, tears rolling down our cheeks.

"Alright, alright," said Jamel. I could see him losing patience with the both of us, but he stayed cool and said calmly, "Connor, what happened tonight? What happened to the car?"

I put on a straight face. "I gave it back to Owen."

He nodded slowly. "Okay. Tell me *how* did you do that."

"I left it at the dealership."

Jack spoke up. "You left it … *in* the dealership." I couldn't help it. I started laughing again, making him chortle.

Ethan was over it. "What the fuck does that mean!?" He raised his voice.

"Connor crashed his car into the dealership!" Jack yelled.

"You did *what!?*" Jamel exclaimed.

"You fucking narc!" I yelled at Jack.

"I'm sorry," Jack snickered, obviously not sorry at all. "But I'm not going down for your shit."

Ethan turned to his husband. "Yeah? Maybe you should have thought of that before you stood to the side and let him drive his car into his father's fucking dealership!"

"He didn't stand to the side; he was in the car with me," I tattled with a smile.

"You fucking narc!" Jack yelled at me, but he was also smiling.

"What the fuck, Jack," Jamel groaned angrily.

Before he could respond, Ethan exploded again. "Are you insane!? You had one job, Jack! Get Connor home safely. Why is it that whenever you have to keep this asshole out of trouble, *you* end up in trouble too?"

"Because he's my best friend. Who else is going to stupid shit with me?" I said innocently. Jack giggled.

"You're a fucking idiot. Do you know that?" Ethan said to me.

"I've been told that from time to time," I said smugly.

"Connor—" Ethan started through gritted teeth.

Jamel touched Ethan's shoulder again. "Alright, alright." I could see he was really trying to keep it together. He opened his mouth to speak, closed it, closed his eyes, clasped his fingers in front of his mouth, then opened his eyes again.

He spoke calmly, but his eyes were blazing mad. "So. You thought it would be a good idea to get drunk and smash your car into your father's dealership, just days after you were sitting on trial for trying to murder him? What if he comes after you again, Connor? For any number of charges that the ADA would be happy to throw at you: defamation of property, reckless endangerment, drunk driving. Did you *think* about any of that at all? Huh?"

I didn't. And I was honest in saying that. "I didn't *think* … at all."

"Obviously!" Ethan yelled at me.

"But I don't regret it," I said loudly and seriously. "And I'm not going to let any of you make me feel bad for shoving one last dildo up his ass." I looked at Jamel who was still visibly angry, but I didn't care. "Take me home, baby."

I turned to Jack and held my arms out. He walked into them, and we hugged tightly. "I love you, Jack." It was the first time I had ever said those words to him. Too little, too late, but it was real, all the same.

"I love you too, Connor," he said back.

I kissed the side of his head and walked out of the Inn. I climbed into Jamel's unlocked truck and closed my eyes. I knew what Jamel said was one hundred percent true, but I just didn't have the wherewithal to care. I felt good. Great. For some reason, I knew Owen wouldn't come after me again. I felt like I was finally free of him, and it was the best feeling ever.

I turned on my phone and I had a series of voice-mails, missed calls and texts. But there was only one text that caught my eye.

[Lovie: Sam said you were drinking a lot tonight. Don't do anything stupid.]

[Connor: Toooooo….late?]

[Lovie: Ugh. You can't go three days without me? You even sound drunk over text.]

[Connor: (;]

[Lovie: I saw your mom today at the post office when I went to visit my folks. She's going to reach out soon. She found a way.]

[Connor: I knew she would. Thanks for letting me know.]

[Lovie: Of course. So, what happened tonight?]

[Connor: Long story.]

[Lovie: Tell me about it tomorrow when you come over and see me and Tykeya. Bring me half a dozen donuts, three glazed, the rest I don't care, and a medium mocha latte, extra mocha.]

[Connor: Only if Ty is okay with it. I will not be the cause of any issues in your marriage.]

[Lovie: Ty and I are fine. We love each other and we'll be fine. You two will never be friends, but you're brothers now. And you're my brother too. And I need my brother to bring me donuts and coffee tomorrow. Don't forget the extra mocha.]

[Connor: Be there in the morning.]

[Lovie: Thank you. Love you, Connor.]

[Connor: Love you too, Lovie.]

I held the phone close to my heart, closed my eyes, and smiled. *It will be different, but I didn't lose her. For that I am grateful.*

I must have fallen asleep because I didn't hear Jamel get into the truck. I heard the key jingle in the ignition and felt the rumbling of the engine. I didn't open my eyes. I just put my head on his shoulder. I felt him put his hand on my thigh and rub it a few times as he drove us home.

❤

My phone went off at 5:17 a.m., the Thursday right before New Year's Eve.

[Mom: Breakfast at the Dove Diner. 8 a.m. Don't be late.]

I exhaled. "Who is it?" Jamel asked groggily.

"My mother. We're having breakfast this morning."

He turned to look at me in the bed, and my face broke into a smile. He kissed my cheek and left the bed to get ready for work. I got ready too and was at the diner by 7:50 a.m., thinking I was getting there early. But she was already there, sitting in our booth.

I slid in across from her and she smiled at me. She reached across the table top and I grabbed her hand. "How is Vinnie Vet Buddies going?" Mom asked.

I told her and we talked for the next two hours about everything except Owen. It was a perfect day.

CHAPTER 13

NOT MY CIRCUS, NOT MY MONKEYS

~~~~January 2013~~~~

"Listen, this is not my circus, and not my monkeys. You're playing ringmaster tonight," Mel said before our guests arrived.

I smiled. "Okay, fine, but remember: I had your back with Donny and your dad."

"Okay. But as long as you don't start any shit tonight," Jamel said. "If you start shit, you're going to drown in it all by yourself."

That made me laugh. I kissed his lips. "As long as he's a good guy, I'll be on my best behavior." He looked at me skeptically but went to get the wine from the basement for our dinner party.

Our doorbell rang just as I was getting the steak out of the oven. Jamel went to answer it.
~~~~

"Hiiiieee!" I heard my sister's voice ring out. Angie was happier now that the trial was over. She was still living on her own with MK as her roommate.

Lavell's girlfriend Kendra was right behind her, along with Lavell and his roommate, Chad. I wasn't sure why Chad decided to tag along, but it was fine since it evened out the guests. And he was a nice guy anyway. He was skinny and kinda geeky-looking, with Clark Kent glasses hiding dark blue eyes. Mary Kate was on her way to introduce me to her boyfriend, some investment banker named Dennis. It was the purpose of this gathering that she insisted on having, probably so I couldn't grill him the way I wanted to with everyone around.

We exchanged hugs and handshakes and the wine was passed around. Angie came into the kitchen. "How are you?" she asked.

I shrugged. "I'm good."

She came closer. "He's not pressing charges. He told the insurance company it was a random attack by a stranger. They pressed him because they knew it was your car, his own son, and at first, they weren't going to pay. But eventually, they agreed to let it go after they dug into the history between you two. The glass is back up, the car is gone, and you won't be bothered by him again."

I nodded. "So, I'm a stranger to him?" She opened her mouth then closed it. I nodded again. "It's okay. He's a stranger to me too." I gave her a smile. "Let's eat."

"Okay, but Connor, there is something else I need to tell you."

"Honestly Angie, I don't give a shit anymore about him and what he says and what he's doing." I began walking away from her.

"No it's … about … me … and…" she trailed off.

The doorbell rang again. "Just tell me later, Ang, okay? Let's get through this dinner without me putting my foot up MK's new boyfriend's ass, then you can tell me all about you."

"Connor, be nice to him, please!?" she pleaded.

"Ang, anybody who is with one of my sisters has to expect the lashing I'm going to give him. He'd better say all the right things." She looked horrified. I left her in the kitchen and went to greet our new guests.

Dennis came in, all smiles. "Hi, everyone! Connor, so good to meet you," he said in a jovial tone. He gave me a firm handshake.

I had to admit, she knew how to pick them. Dennis Anderson was gorgeous. He had a full head of wavy dark hair, olive skin, light brown eyes, full lips, and a nice smile. Dennis was as tall as me and looked like he spent a lot of time in the gym. He had a lively personality, greeted everyone with a smile, hugged Angie like he knew her already, and introduced himself to Lavell, Kendra, and Chad. MK followed him around like a puppy and it was annoying to watch, honestly, but I decided to keep my comments to myself. For now.

For dinner, Angie sat between Kendra and Chad while Lavell sat next to Mary Kate and Dennis, with Jamel and I on opposite ends of the table. Chad carried a lot of the conversation for some reason, making everyone at ease, bringing up various topics and making corny jokes. I found out a bit about him too; he came from a wealthy family but wanted to make it on his own so other than them paying for MIT, he asked his parents for nothing. Instead, he worked a part-time job to pay for his books, essentials, and for his apartment while finishing up his last year. I respected that.

I turned my attention to Mary Kate's boyfriend. Dennis was Boston bred, through and through. He grew up in West Roxbury, attended Boston College, and went to Boston University Questrom School of Business for his MBA. At 27, he was already successful, wealthy, and making a name for himself as one of the youngest investment bankers in the city. His grandmother was Filipino, which was where he got his complexion, and he could speak a little Tagalog. His father was from Wales originally, and he can also speak a little Welsh too. He also spoke a little Spanish and Mandarin. I knew all of this because the guy wouldn't stop talking. He was definitely a salesman.

"So," I began as dinner was wrapping up. "How did you and MK meet?"

My sister began, "Well I was—"

But Dennis cut her off. "He asked me, honey."

"Oh, sorry!" she said quickly.

My eyes narrowed at her and her submissive demeanor. "Her company, Adobe Marketing, was doing some work with our firm when I passed by the conference room, and I saw her. I took one look at her and I thought—with all due respect, Connor—that she is *baaaad!*" He smiled at me, but I didn't smile back. "I mean, really, she's the most beautiful girl I've ever seen. I kept walking past the glass windows, just waiting for her to notice me, but she never looked up."

"Oh, I noticed," she spoke up again. "Black Tom Ford suit, Salvatore Ferragamo shoes, MontBlanc TimeWalker watch? Oh, I definitely noticed." She touched his arm.

He smiled at her and then turned back to me. "So, I waited for their first break, and I went up to her and said, 'You're gorgeous. I need your name, your number, and to take you out to dinner tonight.'"

I resisted the urge to roll my eyes as I watched my sister gush over this story. "It was so romantic, right out of a fairy tale."

"But you didn't say yes, honey," Dennis reminded her. "You laughed and walked away."

"Of course not. I needed to play hard-to-get," she said slyly.

He looked back up at me. "After she walked away, I did some digging. I went to their company directory and found her name. I went to her social media pages to find out the things she likes and sent gifts to her home and flowers to her office for a week. On Friday, I showed up at her work in a limo and told her, 'I'm taking you out, honey. And I will not be refused.'"

MK gushed, "I mean, how could I refuse that?"

They leaned in and kissed like no one was watching them. I glanced at Jamel. I knew we were thinking the same thing: *What kinda 50 Shades of Grey shit is this?*

I couldn't help it. "Soooooo, you stalked my sister?"

They both looked up at me sharply. He responded, "No, I… no."

"Connor, stop it," Mary Kate jumped in. "He didn't stalk me; he … *pursued* me."

I raised an eyebrow at her. "Pursued you? He found out your name, where you worked, and where you lived. If he was a serial killer, you'd be dead by now."

"I didn't stalk her," Dennis said earnestly. "I just wanted to let her know that I was taking notice of her, and I would do anything to make her mine."

"Kinda sounds like stalking to me," Chad mumbled from across the table. Angie swatted his arm and he chuckled. Dennis glared at him. But then he turned his attention back to me.

"Connor, I—"

"Shut up," I said sternly. "I was talking to my sister, *honey*." I set my eyes back on MK. "Who are you right now?" I asked her. "Mom?"

"What does that mean?"

"You know what that means."

"Dennis isn't like that," she argued.

"He stalked you. He tells you what to do. He shuts you up when he's talking. Who does that sound like?"

"Maybe this isn't the time or place to have this conversation," Jamel said quietly.

"Dennis isn't like that!" she yelled at me. "He's kind and generous, and he would never, *ever* hurt me."

"Isn't it always like that in the beginning, *honey*?" I said sarcastically.

My little sister stood up. "And it's going to be like that in the end because we're getting married!"

My mouth dropped open. *She can't be fucking serious.*

Dennis reached out and touched her arm. He actually pulled on her arm a little to get her to sit her down, and I really didn't like that. "It's okay. Calm down, honey. I can speak for myself. No more yelling."

When she was seated, he turned to me. "Connor, I have the utmost respect for you. For your service and bravery. For the way you love and take care of everyone in your life. For being who you are, without apologies. I've been waiting to meet you for a long time, but Mary Kate said that with the trial and all, it wasn't the right time."

I sat back and let this salesman try to smooth-talk me.

"I know about your family's history and childhood, and I understand your concerns," he continued. "Mary Kate told me everything. Now, I'm a God-fearing man, a proud conservative, and I expect the natural order of man as the head of the household, and the woman as the submissive wife. But there are some things that I would never do, starting with ever putting my hands on a woman, ever belittling her, ever hurting her in any way. My role as the man, and husband, is to love and uplift my wife and children. These are the things my father instilled in me. You have my word, in front of everyone here, to hold me accountable: what you experienced growing up would never happen in our relationship.

"I love Mary Kate. Yes, at first, I was attracted to her beauty. And then I became attracted to her personality, her courage, her love of God's creatures, great and small, her God-fearing spirit. She's everything that I've ever wanted in this life. She will be my wife, and my responsibility, from this moment on. You do not have to worry. I will take care of her. And I will never hurt her."

I stared at him, not sure if he was bullshitting me. "Mom and Owen know you're getting married?" I asked Mary Kate.

He spoke before she could. "Yes, they know. I asked Owen for her hand in marriage in November, and we were engaged on New Year's Eve. You're the last member of the family to know."

I slowly turned my eyes back to him. "So, you speak for her now, huh?"

"I do," Dennis said bravely.

I leaned into the table and said, "Okay, hear this. The day my sister comes to me to tell me that you accidentally pushed or hit her, the day I see a bruise on her body that's not supposed to be there, the moment I find out that you've been calling her a cunt, a bitch, a worthless piece of shit, stupid, ugly, or any degrading word that breaks down her spirit, the *second* I see unhappy tears on her face that you caused for any fucking reason, I will put a bullet in your chest in broad daylight. You have my word in front of everyone here. I was ready to kill my own father. You're nothing to me. Remember that."

I leaned back and added, "Now, go on and live your happy life."

It was deadly silent at the table. I didn't take my eyes off of him, letting him know I wasn't fucking around. *The cycle of abuse will not continue in my family.*

To his credit, he didn't flinch, but I saw the fear in his eyes. He swallowed, then said, "You have my word." I gave him a small nod.

Mary Kate exploded. "What the entire FUCK, Connor!?"

Jamel tried to intervene. "Mary Kate, listen—"

She stood up again. "No, fuck *that*, Jamel! He does not get to go around threatening to kill people, especially the man that I love! Because you know what? I'm not Katherine. And he's not Owen. And just because you see two people living more conservatively than you and Jamel does not mean it's wrong. It's what I want. Denny is what I want! So, whether you like it or not, I will be a submissive wife, a stay-at-home mom with four children and a husband who loves and honors me as the Bible commands us to!"

I raised an eyebrow but said nothing.

She sat back down and then said with a flick of her wrist, "Oh, and make sure you give that same bullshit speech to Chad over there!"

It took me a moment to realize what she meant, especially after Angie exploded. "What the *fuck*, Mary Kate!" she cried.

"I'm sorry, but there is no way I am going through this alone," MK retorted. "It's your turn."

I slowly turned to the two of them on the other side of me. Angie looked fearful, but it did not compare to Chad. He practically turned green, his chin quivering. *That poor nerdy bastard.*

I started laughing. "Holy shit." I laughed louder, putting my hand on my head. "Holy. Shit."

"Connor," Angie started hesitantly. "Connor, please. We just… it… Chad and I, we're … new and we're just … figuring it all out. Right, Chad?"

She looked at him for confirmation. He couldn't even speak. It looked as if he opened his mouth, vomit would pour out. "Connor, please," Angie said again, turning back to me when she realized that Chad would not be giving me an *I'm the man in this relationship* speech. This was definitely not a patriarchal relationship. That just made me laugh even more.

"Did you know?" I asked Jamel, who looked amused.

He shook his head. "Not my circus, not my monkeys." Then he started a deep belly laugh, which just kept me laughing. *I love that man.*

Kendra and Lavell were also chuckling. I guess only half the people at the table found the whole situation hilarious. Since Lavell and Angie met about seven months ago, she had been hanging out in Boston a lot. I just assumed they had gotten really close. But apparently, I had missed all of the signs. It was to hang out with Chad. Wonderful.

When I got myself together, I looked at my baby sister. "Okay. How long has this been official?"

"Since the housewarming in September. Remember, you couldn't go because..."

I nodded. "Okay." I took a sip of wine.

"Oh, he doesn't get the 'I'll put a bullet in your chest in broad daylight' threat?" Mary Kate asked angrily.

I shrugged. "Don't need to. He knows it applies to him too." I looked at him. "You know it applies to you too, right?" I asked seriously. He nodded profusely, still unable to speak. "Good." I stood up. "Who wants dessert? I picked up a couple of fresh apple pies from Frazier Orchards." I went into the kitchen.

CHAPTER 14

THAT'S PRIDE

~~~~ June 2013 ~~~

"What did you dream about?" she asked me.

I hesitated but answered honestly. "My first time with Jack." She nodded, wanting me to go on. "Halloween, 2000. They were having a party. I was sixteen, and I went over to his house to apologize to him for…" I sighed. "Doesn't matter."

"It does," CJ said right away. "Everything you say matters, Connor."

I smiled at her. *She's so affirming.* Dr. Cynthia Johns-Mero was a psych professor at Rhode Island University. She was a retired Air Force Technical Sergeant and helped many people figure out their life goals while in the service. She left the military in 2011, after Don't Ask Don't Tell was repealed, to marry her longtime girlfriend, Senior Airwoman Enriqa Mero, who was still
~~~~

in the service. CJ became a therapist with her own practice. My therapist.

I took what the judge said seriously. I found a therapist to help me work through my trauma. I wanted someone who had military experience and was gay, so they understood where I was coming from right from the beginning. Jack recommended her to me. He took her five-week course on Dialectical Behavioral Therapy and how to apply it to all different types of disorders, not just Borderline Personality Disorder or substance abuse. They'd kept in touch and when I casually mentioned that I wanted to try therapy, he immediately gave me her number. "I've been waiting for you to ask," he'd said.

Six months after the trial, a month before my 29th birthday, there I was in another bi-weekly visit. CJ and I had been talking about my sexual history, my feelings around coming out, and my insecurities. She knew about the trial, and the abuse, but had yet to ask any questions. We started with where I was at that moment and have slowly been making our way backward.

"What happened between you and Jack that you went to his house to apologize?"

"I let Jack go down on me and then I went down on him, my first time ever giving a blow job. I … loved it. Loved." She nodded and stayed silent. She was good at that, staying quiet and letting me get it all out. "I loved everything about it, the feel, the taste, the way he moaned. When he came, I held it in my mouth for a moment…" I closed my eyes and remembered. "I held his cum in my mouth before I swallowed it and it felt … so fucking amazing. And then it hit me why it felt so right, why it made me so hard, going down on him. It was a dull thought in the back of my head that became a scream in my ears."

"And that thought was…?"

I opened my eyes. "That I'm gay. Not even bi, but gay. I wanted to do this with boys. I wanted to do this with him."

"Was that the first time you said it to yourself?" she asked. "Think as far back as you can."

I was thoughtful. "I think it was. Even though I knew I was attracted to him, I still didn't think I was actually gay. We had been fooling around for a few weeks by then, almost every day. Sure, I thought he was gorgeous and was a good kisser. But was I sexually attracted to him? I don't think I knew for sure until then. Until I went down on him. Then I knew for sure. I wanted to fuck him, but even more than that, I wanted him to fuck me. And there is no other reason for me to want a boy to put his dick in me if I wasn't completely gay."

CJ shrugged. "You could have been bisexual. It would have been perfectly normal for you to be sexually attracted to both sexes."

"But after that moment, I knew for sure what I was. I visualized a future together, and Owen killing us both for it. And it scared the shit out of me. So, I did the complete opposite. I told him I wasn't gay, that I was done with him, and to get lost. I kicked him out of my bed and my house. I hurt him. Badly."

"I understand," she said. "You rejected him when he was at his most vulnerable, to avoid being vulnerable yourself. Instead of talking to him about your fears, you pushed him away."

I was thoughtful again. "Yeah. Yeah, I guess I did."

"And then you went to apologize to him. Why?"

"Because I didn't mean to hurt him."

"But you did," she challenged me. "You said so yourself, that you did the opposite of what you were feeling. You rejected him on purpose, so he wouldn't see who you really were. And it's a pattern for you that still continues: pushing people away instead of talking about your feelings."

She let me sit in my discomfort. I hated that she was right. I hated being reminded of what an asshole I was to him.

"Okay," I finally said. "I meant to hurt him. But then I felt like shit afterward. He wouldn't look at me, wouldn't let me apologize for weeks. I thought about him day and night. I started a fight with my girlfriend at the time just so that I could break up with her. At school, I tried to tell him that I'd broken up with her, but he wouldn't talk to me. And it was breaking my heart."

"Tell me why you went to his home that day. Be honest with yourself."

"I needed to see him. I needed to be around him. I needed him to forgive me and … I wanted him."

"And you got him," she said with a smirk.

I smirked back. "I sure fucking did."

"Why do you think you dreamed that particular dream? Was it about Jack?"

I shook my head. "It wasn't about Jack. I don't think about Jack in that way anymore. It was about me. It was the realization that I've always been this person."

"Yes, but I think it's deeper than that," she challenged me again. "When you gave in to your desire for Jack, how did it feel?"

"Freeing," I said without thinking.

"So, for the first time you felt free. Free to be who you are."

"Yeah. Yeah, I guess so."

"Don't guess," she said sternly. "Do you know or don't you?"

I smiled at her again. "Yes. It was the first time I felt absolutely free to give in to what I really wanted and discover who I am."

She tapped her fingers on her leg while watching me. "Do you still feel free? Like, right now, do you feel free to be you?"

"With you in this room? Yes."

"And outside of this room?"

"At home with Jamel, yes."

"And outside of your home? At work? Does the little rainbow sticker that Ethan put on the leasing door still bother you?"

I sighed. "I try not to think about it too much."

"How many times a day do you glance up at it?" she asked.

"I don't know," I said, looking down at my fingers. "Probably once an hour."

She didn't say anything. She let me sit in my discomfort again. After a long moment, I asked, "Why do I still feel ashamed of it?"

She replied, "Because too many signs in this world tell us to be ashamed of who we are. That we are wrong for feeling what we feel. You're not the problem. Society is. And we have to fight against that negative voice every single day, tell it to shut the fuck up, and carry on with our heads held high. That's pride. Pride is not about the parades, and parties, and painting rainbows on our faces. It's not about finding men to fuck in the back of the club or a dark alley. This right here: fighting against that negative voice, living your life, loving who you love. *That's* pride, Connor."

I stared at my hands. She let me sit in my thoughts. Before Jamel, I would spend Pride Month trying to fuck every single man that glanced my way. My blow job count would go up considerably. But Mel's presence in my life changed all that, and I didn't realize it until just then. The first year Jamel and I were together, I had moved out of my parents' house that June. The second year, we bought a house and worked on it together. Last June, I came out to my parents.

Jamel is a proud gay man. There is no doubt about that. I watch his face light up every year around this time. Suddenly, rainbow flags appear in shops and on cars and he just smiles while I cringe. This is the first year that we get to celebrate pride together as a couple: out, loud, and proud. And I don't know if I can do that.

I told her what I was feeling. "What if I can't be who he needs me to be? What if I can't be loud and proud?"

CJ sighed and leaned forward. "You asked me two questions. I'm going to ask you two counter questions. You're ready? Look at me, Connor."

"Yeah." I looked up.

"One, who do you think Jamel needs you to be?"

"Someone who's not ashamed of who he is," I said right away.

"Do you think Jamel has never felt ashamed or humiliated? Do you think no one in his life has ever made him feel like shit for being a gay? For being black? For being proud of both?"

She got me. "Of course Jamel has experience discrimination," I answered. "We've had some incidents together."

She asked, "Has Jamel given you any indication that he needs you to be a flamboyant gay man, hugging and kissing in public, waving a rainbow flag, yelling 'Happy Pride' like these drunk idiots out there?"

I smiled at her. "That's more than two questions."

She smiled back. "Answer the question."

I shook my head. "No. Never. He has always been patient with me."

"Why can't you be patient with yourself?"

I opened my mouth, then closed it. Eventually I mumbled, "I don't know."

"You just came out, Connor. You're a baby in all this. Crawl before you walk. You're exactly where you need to be, getting to know who you are, learning to love yourself like you've never loved yourself before. And, like you've acknowledged to me, you have a lot of support around you, a lot of people who love you. A lot of people who can help you on this journey. And it is a lifelong journey, trust me."

"I just feel like … it's Pride Month. He's a proud gay man, and technically, I'm out. I need to show him that

I'm proud of being gay too. Even if it's not entirely … true." I cringed.

CJ didn't flinch. "Let's look at it differently. You love him. So why don't you do something to show him that? Just quietly celebrate your relationship. That's pride too."

I was thoughtful. "That's a good idea."

She shrugged. "I get good ideas from time to time." She winked at me and I smiled at her.

"So where are we going?" Jamel asked.

"You'll see when we get there," I said slyly.

He smiled and sat back in my all-white Toyota 4Runner. Lovie went with me to pick it out a few days after I kindly gave the Infiniti Q50 back to Owen. I specifically did not want an American car, and she liked the way this one drove, so I financed it.

On the last weekend of the month, I told him that I was taking him out on a date, so to look fancy. When I pulled up at the restaurant, he smiled. Gianni's Bistro was where we had our first date.

When we approached the hostess, I pointed to a booth toward the back. "Can we have that table?"

"Certainly." She grabbed the menus, and we followed her to the booth. It was where we first met.

Jamel sat down across from me. "So, what's the occasion?" he asked.

I looked at the little flags on the table and picked up the rainbow one. I waved it a little and sang softly, "Happy Priiiide."

Mel laughed out loud. He put his hand over mine and said softly back, "Happy Pride."

We ordered a bottle of Riesling for the table. I had the chicken and shrimp alfredo, and he had the sausage and gnocchi. We ate and talked about random things, like how Donny was settling in living in Richmond, twenty minutes away from Vanessa and his son, and how Mary Kate was driving Angie crazy with planning the wedding that was set for August 8th, which she found out was Happiness Day.

I told him about the next phase of Vinnie's Vet Buddies. "There is a trauma conference coming up in the fall in Chicago and the organizers reached out to me to do the keynote on veterans and trauma. Benjin and I are going to do it together. Then we want to start putting together our own mini workshops across the country. Different topics geared toward providers working with vets, and for vets that just need to connect with other vets."

"It sounds great, Connor. I support this one hundred percent," he said sincerely.

"Even if it means we'll be apart more?" I questioned. "I'll be doing a lot of traveling, at least four times a year, starting next year."

"Are you worried about that? Being away from me?" he asked.

"It's just… We've never really been apart. It'll be hard on both of us. It may challenge our relationship a little."

He was thoughtful in his answer to me. "Remember when we first got together, and you thought I was going back into the Army? Do you remember what you said to me?"

I smiled. "That I'm not some little, pussy ass bitch?"

He chuckled. "That we'll make it work. And if we were determined to make it work then, we are definitely motivated to make it work now. Live your dream, Connor. Your work is your passion, and I want you to see it through. I'm always going to be here."

My heart exploded with love for him. "You've always believed in me. From the last time we sat here together until now, you've never stopped believing in me."

He leaned into the table and said seriously, "I'm your biggest Journey fan." That made me laugh out loud at his corny ass joke. He chuckled too.

When the bill came, I casually put my credit card in the pocket, then handed it back to the waiter. My Act of Service for him. "I'm taking you out. Next time, you'll take me out." I winked at him.

Jamel smiled and touched my hand. "Gonna take me home now?"

I played with his fingers. "Not yet. There's a place I want to take you that's not too far from here."

"Hmmm…." was his only response.

We exited the restaurant and left the car in the parking lot. We walked side by side. I reached over and grabbed his hand without looking at him. I caught a glimpse of his smirk, and he turned his hand so that our fingers intertwined. I tried not to be nervous, but as usual, Jamel made me feel safe. He casually moved his thumb back and forth against my skin as we walked about five minutes into downtown Providence.

Some people noticed us, but no one gave us a nasty look. Another male couple walked toward us, in their own world, holding hands, laughing and talking loudly. Watching them made me smile.

One of them noticed my grin. Before I could turn away, he greeted us. "Hey there, guys!"

"Hey," I happily responded. We smiled at each other as they kept walking and laughing together.

I turned to Jamel and he was watching me. I bumped my shoulder against his. He kissed my cheek and I immediately turned red. He chuckled and squeezed my hand. I squeezed it back and took him across the street to the Tiki Lounge.

"It's a bar I used to go to, way back when," I explained as I opened the door for us. "I wanted to take you here, experience it with you as a cou—"

"Connor!" the man behind the counter yelled.

I looked over at him. "Do I know you?"

"Damon!" he yelled again and stood up. "It's me, Damon!"

"Oh." I stared at him then said nonchalantly, "Hi."

He hesitated, looked at Jamel, and sat back down. He mumbled, "Um… hi. Twenty for singles. Thirty for couples."

I handed him two twenty-dollar bills; he handed us two rubber rainbow armbands. "Keep the change." We put on our armbands, and I pulled Jamel into the bar with me without looking back.

The place was crowded as we approached the bar. It was decorated with rainbow flags, which wasn't uncommon for the last Saturday in June. I waited until the 6'5" Italian bartender caught my eye. "Well look what the cat dragged in!!" he chortled. Vidal came over to us and I reached my hand out. He slapped my palm twice in greeting.

"I thought you died, man," he joked. "That would have been the only thing to keep you from here on Friday nights."

I laughed out loud. "Vidal, this is my boyfriend, Jamel." I yelled over the music and noise. "Jamel, this is Vidal. The owner of this shithole."

Vidal's eyes went wide. "Boyfriend!? Get the fuck outta here!"

I raised my hands in a mock shrug and smiled. "Three and a half years and counting."

"Three years!?" he yelled again. "No wonder you haven't shown your face around here." Vidal turned to Jamel and touched his shoulder. "Your first drink is on me, whatever you want. You earned it for trapping this asshole."

Jamel laughed a big laugh. "Anything with Henny in it."

"You got it, my man." He gave Jamel a dap then turned back to me. "You look good, Connor. Happy." I grinned at him. Vidal was someone who helped me get comfortable in gay bars early on and became a really good friend.

"Island Henny and Tequila Paloma coming right up!" he yelled, reaching for the bottle of Hennessey.

Jamel and I turned to the crowd as our drinks were being made and people watched. It was definitely not my scene anymore. *Is it me or is everyone in here five to ten years younger?* Jamel was getting stared at left and right, like I wasn't standing right next to him. It made me move closer, so that our shoulders touched.

The muscular man dancing in a sparkly thong on the platform looked over at me and smiled widely. I recognized him and raised my hand to say hello. He winked and continued dancing. Jamel looked over at him, then at me and smirked. I smiled then cringed, making him laugh out loud.

Vidal tapped my shoulder when he placed the drinks down and we grabbed our cups. "Good seeing you, Connor," he said. "Don't be a stranger. Bring Jamel around more often." He gave Jamel another dap and moved on.

"Cheers to us," I said, holding out my cup to him. "And to having pride in our relationship."

"Cheers, baby." We tapped our cups and drank, staring at each other. "So. Tell me about young Damon out there."

I rolled my eyes and turned away. "C'mon, man. You don't want to hear about that." I put my back to the bar and sipped casually.

He also leaned against the bar. "I think I do," he said back just as casually.

I took a long time to answer as I looked around. I thought I saw Officer Pike, but he looked different somehow. I glanced at Jamel, who was waiting for me to talk. He knew I would.

"Damon was a barely 18-year-old twink who had no idea what he was doing. I took his virginity, showed him the basics, and dropped him. Last time I saw him, I came on his face in the back room of Alley Cat, pissed on him, then told him to get lost." Jamel blinked, his face impassive.

I turned my body toward him. "I was an asshole and a user. I'm not proud of it. But it's who I was. That's my honesty."

Jamel nodded. "Thank you for your honesty." He touched my chin and kissed my lips.

"I thought that was you," a voice behind Jamel said.

I turned toward the voice. "Officer Pike." I shook his hand. "You're cuter out of uniform."

Even in the dimmed lights, I saw him blush. "It's Pete." He stared at me and then remembered his manners. "And this is Warren, my partner."

Warren was brown-skinned, about the same height and build as Pete, with dark eyes and a full beard. I shook his hand too. Then Warren stared at Jamel so intently, like he was itching to be introduced. It made me want to reach over and smack his face.

Instead, I touched my boyfriend's arm. "This is Jamel, but you've met already," I said to the cop. Jamel looked confused as he shook Pete and Warren's hands. "Officer Pike—Pete—was one of the men that arrested me that night at the house," I reminded him.

"Oooh," he said in recognition.

"Yeah, you were a little too angry to notice me," Pete said with a chuckle.

"No, I remember. You're the one that pulled your gun on me," he said as if we were discussing paint colors.

"Um… yeah." There was an awkward silence and then he said to me, "I followed your trial, saw it was hung. I guess the ADA let it go, huh?"

"Looks like he did." I shrugged.

"Good. I'm happy for you. Well ah… stay out of trouble." He winked at me.

I smiled at him. "Don't worry. Jamel keeps me out of trouble." I winked back.

"You're in the military?" Warren suddenly asked.

We both turned to Warren, but he wasn't talking to me. I realized he was still staring at Jamel, like neither Pete nor I were there. I gave Jamel an amused look, but Jamel wouldn't look at me.

"I was, an Army Sergeant. I'm retired now," Jamel answered.

"I could tell. I'm in the Navy. I teach at the Naval Justice School in Newport."

I almost rolled my eyes. But then Jamel smiled. "Navy, huh? I thought about going into the Navy at one point." He stretched out his arm and showed Warren his compass tattoo. And the asshole had the audacity to touch my boyfriend's arm, right in front of me.

"This is really nicely done," he said.

"Thanks," Jamel replied.

Okay, I've had enough of this. I stretched out my hand across Jamel's arm so that Warren would let go. "It's really nice to meet you, Warren." I gave him a hard look.

Warren smiled and shook my hand. Pete smiled too, took Warren's hand, and led him away.

I turned to Jamel, whose face was unreadable. "What was *that*?"

"What was what?" he asked innocently.

I narrowed my eyes at him. "Flirting with Warren? You know he wants you."

"Jealous?" he asked with amusement.

"Nope," I lied. "Fuck the Navy," I added with spite.

Mel chuckled. "The cop wants you. And you were definitely flirting with him."

"Jealous?" I teased him, taking a sip of my drink.

He shook his head. "Of pee pee? Nope."

I almost spit out my drink. "Pee pee!?"

"C'mon. Peter Pike? P. P.? He definitely got called pee pee growing up."

I laughed out loud and kissed my man on the lips. "Let's get out of here before we run into someone else I know. Or slept with."

"You mean other than Damon, Hercules over there, and Vidal?" he asked with a twinkle in his eye.

I opened my mouth and then closed it, making him laugh out loud again. "Was this a bad idea bringing you here?" I asked seriously.

"Not at all," he said. "It's nice seeing you in your element. I don't get to see this side of you. It's fascinating."

"Well, you get a side of me that no one else has." I reached up and caressed the nape of his neck. "The loving side. The affectionate side."

"I'm loving all these signs of affection you're giving me," he said as he pulled me closer.

"Well, you're worth it," I said on his lips. "You've been giving me signs of affection from our first date."

We kissed softly, sweetly, swaying to the music that was fading into the background. We ended up staying a little longer, dancing together.

After a couple of songs, I murmured, "Take me home, Big Daddy."

He kinda growled and kissed me forcefully. Then he took my hand and we walked through the crowd.

At the entrance, I turned back to Damon who was avoiding my eyes. "Hey, Damon," I called out to him. "Did you ever do the Coast Guard like we talked about?"

His eyes lit up in surprise. "Yeah… yeah. I'm in the Reserves, two weekends a month, one week a year."

"That's awesome. I told you that you would love it." He smiled pridefully at me. "It's good seeing you, Damon. You look good."

"Thanks. You too," he replied, happy that I acknowledged him this time. Jamel gently tugged my hand and I followed him out of the bar.

We walked back in silence. This time, I tried not to notice who was looking our way. It was only when we got into my truck, and I put my hand on the steering wheel, that I realized I still had my rainbow armband on. I had unknowingly slid it over my right hand, and it fit well over the tattooed armband; only Vinnie's initials were visible, as if attached to the rainbow armband. I rubbed the VB and smiled, lost in thought before I realized I never actually started the car. I looked up and Jamel was watching me with a small smile on his face.

"Sorry," I mumbled, turning the key in the ignition.

"For what?" he asked. "He gets to celebrate Pride too."

I looked over at my partner and felt the tears pool in my eyes; I blinked them away. I grabbed his hand, kissed his knuckles, and began to drive us home.

I held his hand the whole way.

❤

We parked and came inside through the garage. He started to go up the stairs to the kitchen, but I took his hand and led him to the media room instead. Our night wasn't done yet. I dimmed the lights, then picked up the remote and pressed play. Sade's "Cherish The Day" began to play loudly, one of his favorite songs. He gave me a small smile as I pulled him close and sang the song to him.

I connected my fingers around his neck and he held me close. We swayed to the music, kissing softly. "It's you and me, baby. For life," I whispered in his ear.

He pulled back to look in my face and nodded. I slid my hands from his neck down his chest and began to unbutton his shirt. He let me, watching me with hunger in his eyes. Once I slid his shirt off, he shucked my shirt up and over my head. He turned me around and pulled me back against him, his hairy chest on my bare back. As we swayed to the music, I rolled my hips against his groin. He slowly unbuckled my belt and unzipped my jeans. He reached down and caressed the length of me. I closed my eyes and let him work me, one hand over my briefs, the other caressing my nipples. His lips and tongue explored my neck.

Suddenly, he let me go, put both hands on my shoulders, and coaxed me to my knees. I happily obliged, my back to him as I heard him unbuckle his own jeans and waited for him to approach me from behind. I felt his cock caress my cheek, smearing pre-cum on my skin. With my eyes still closed, I began to stroke him. I slowly turned around and put him in my mouth. He held onto my shoulders, and I lifted my head and took him all the way into my throat until his pubes tickled my lips. He held me there, watched me watching him, then slowly pulled back to the head. He went down my throat again, and again, and again, and I let him until he gave up first, pulling back with a, "Fuck!"

He was panting and I was not. He dropped to his knees and kissed me aggressively, and I allowed it. As secure as he was in us, something about coming face to face tonight with old lovers and others that desired us had Jamel feeling like he needed to dominate me, stake his claim, remind me of who I belonged to. *But he doesn't need to. I know where my home is, and Jamel is home.*

I grabbed his face with both hands and looked him in the eyes. I needed him to know, to see, that no one else had ever had me like he did, and no one ever will. He opened his mouth to say something, but then didn't.

Instead, he whispered, "I need you."

I nodded. "I know," I said softly. "Make love to me."

I sucked on his bottom lip, then his top lip before I put my tongue in his mouth. I pulled him on top of me and stretched across our basement room floor. He kissed my neck and down my torso, taking off my pants and underwear. He stood up and went to the bathroom as I laid there naked, listening to "Bullet Proof Soul" play. He was back within moments, naked, with the lube we kept down there in hand. Jamel moved incredibly slow, licking my nipples, the creases in between my abs, the crease at my groin. I moaned and squirmed underneath him as he used his tongue to show me how much he wanted me, needed me. He even sucked my toes, kissed up my legs, and licked the inside of my thighs. He greedily sucked my balls, leaving my cock untouched, skin tight, slit leaking.

He stretched out below me and lifted my bottom off the floor with both hands until my hole was completely visible. He pressed his tongue in, out, and around my pucker until my thighs began to shake. Only then did he add the lube and climb over me.

He inserted just the head inside and kissed me deeply, and incredibly slowly, sunk himself inside of me. He moved back and forth at a steady pace, with his mouth on my mouth, neck, and ears. I moaned, keeping my legs open and apart. I became a completely submissive bottom for him, no shit-talking or moving. I didn't touch myself to control my orgasm either. I let it happen naturally. I came first and he pulled all the way out. He turned me over and kissed along my spine down to my bottom before biting the right cheek, making me giggle, then bit me on the left. He added more lube to us both and entered me once more. I stretched out completely and let him take me again, let him have full control over my body, just like he controlled my heart.

He didn't move any faster than when we were face to face, and every ten minutes or so he would pull all the way out and kiss and lick me all over. He wanted to prolong the experience for the both of us. It was reminiscent of the first time we made love, with so much passion and need between us. We made love for so long that "Cherish the Day" started again, and he really needed to release.

"God... oh God..." He moaned into my hair.

I felt his thighs tense up, and he gave me three quick pumps, slowed down and moaned out my name, "Cooooonooooor." I felt every shot deep inside of me with his thrusts, not stopping until he was completely emptied out. He collapsed on top of me.

I didn't move. I laid still, feeling his fast heartbeat on my back, his breath on my neck. When he came back down from his orgasm and his breathing returned to normal, he turned my head, nuzzled his nose with mine and we kissed. He began to move again, although he wasn't completely hard, and reached below me for my aching cock. My eyes fluttered at his touch as he jerked me off until I cried out and came in his hand and onto the blue and brown threads of our carpet.

He slowly pulled out but laid his head on my back, keeping me warm, making me feel safe and secure. We laid there quietly, listening to Sade.

I thought he had fallen asleep when I said, "I love you, Jamel Jones."

But he answered me back, "And I love you, Connor Adrian McIntyre."

"You really aren't going anywhere, are you?" I asked softly.

"No," he replied softly back. "I'm really not. You're my family, my number one priority. My heart. My soul. My reason. My everything. Our love is strong. Our bond is unbreakable. I'll never leave you, Connor. It's you and me, for life."

My heart swelled. Two people from vastly different worlds who happened to walk into the same pharmacy at the same time became this amazing love affair. All the drama I had been through, all the heartache he had been through, and there we were: together and in love. One heart, one soul, and nothing and no one was ever going to break our unbreakable bond.

I let a few tears fall out of my eyes. "Same, Jamel. Same," I replied softly.

I could tell he had a lot on his mind. Jamel was typically quiet, but after going through the mail he was unusually sullen.

"What's wrong?" I asked him at dinner.

"Nothing, just that the premium for Obamacare is going up, again." Jamel sighed. "It's like paying a car note. But what can I do? Especially since that asshole in the White House is trying to get rid of it altogether. If I didn't have a family history of heart disease, then I would just let it go, but I need annual checkups, including cardiology."

"I know. But I told you I would just put you on my insurance," I reminded him. "It allows for domestic partnership. Which we are in."

He smiled. "I might just take you up on that now. But that would be more money coming out of your paycheck."

And here we go again, him worried about my finances. "I can afford it, Mel. It's fine. I just got my open enroll- ment package so it will start next month."

"Okay," he finally agreed.

I had been working for Ethan for about five years already. Three years ago, he finally put together a health insurance package for his employees. I enrolled in the health insurance every year, but there were other things in the package that I had never thought about doing.

"Also in my enrollment package are questions about beneficiaries and accidental death insurance stuff. Stuff I never bothered to fill out in the last couple of years. But I can fill it out now. And maybe put together a living will, giving you permission to pull the plug."

Jamel chuckled. "I have one, a living will," he told me. "My parents are the beneficiaries. It's probably still active."

I didn't like that idea at all. I cocked my head to the side. "If something were to happen to you, your parents would be making the decisions?"

He shrugged. "Yeah. We should probably change that."

He laughed but I was serious. "Yeah, we should. We need to. And I need one too. One that says that you, and only you, should be making decisions for me."

"I agree," he said seriously. "We can write it up and get it notarized. But it might not be legally binding if anyone from either of our families challenges it."

"Because we aren't blood-related?"

"Yeah, because I think they look to the closest living relative to make those kinds of decisions. But let's draw up all the paperwork, anyway. We can have Ethan's lawyer look at it and seal it up airtight. It will be fine," Jamel said nonchalantly.

I don't like that idea either. Mel and I are building a life together. I'm not blood-related, but I am his closest living relative. And he's mine. God forbid something does happen. With Ty and I still in this weird vortex of not-friends-but-family, he would have more control and power over what happens with Jamel than I would. No, that can't happen. But there is only one other way to seal it airtight...

Even I couldn't believe the words as they came out of my mouth: "Or. We could just. You know. Get married. And then there would be no question."

I stared down at my plate as I spoke. I figured Jamel would just look at me stoically or laugh, but he did the unexpected. He looked like he almost choked on his mashed potatoes, then he slowed down his chewing. I watched him swallow, put his spoon down, take a sip of wine, lean back, and give me a tight-lipped smile.

"What?" I asked, trying to appear casual.

"Nothing. I'm just listening to you explain the best way to ensure that I be the one to pull the plug," Jamel said, amused.

Fuck, he's going to milk this one. "Ugh, Jameeeeellll."

He laughed. But he was clearly waiting for me to continue. So I turned my body to him and said, "Okay, I'm just saying, instead of going through the rigmarole of getting papers drawn up, if we have a marriage certificate then everything I have, including my pension, goes to you. As spouses, you'll be my closest living relative so you can make decisions for me if I can't. And vice versa. It just makes sense."

He blinked. "To get married."

"Yes."

"So you want to get married." It was more of a statement than a question.

"If you think ... it's a good idea then yeah, sure."

"Actually, this is your idea." Jamel raised one eyebrow. "All yours."

I rolled my eyes at him. "Okay Mel, fine. My idea. But you're on board, right?"

Jamel smiled again. "On board with marrying you?"

"Yeeeeaaah…?"

He was being weird, so I honestly did not know what he was thinking. Jamel was still smirking, but suddenly he stopped. He shrugged and picked up his spoon to start eating again. "Whatever you want to do, Con."

I watched him for a moment, unsure of what his reaction meant. *Does he want to do this or not?* "Um... okay. Well maybe tomorrow you can drive past the Providence courthouse on the way to work—"

"Oh, no. I'm not doing any of that," Jamel said. "This is *your* idea. You go down to the courthouse, set everything up. Just tell me when and where."

I pouted. "Why not?"

"Because Connor," Jamel put his spoon down again. "When we made the decision to be together, it was me pursuing you, convincing you that we would be perfect together. When we decided to buy this house and move in together, it was my idea. I had to convince you that it would be a great decision. Two major decisions in our relationship and I did the work. This is your idea. Your major decision. It's your turn to do the work."

My mouth opened slightly. I had no idea Jamel felt that way. "Um... okay," I said softly. Mel nodded and continued to eat his dinner.

Okay, so he's on board as long as I set it up and take the lead. But how real does this need to be?

"Soooooo... do you want me to like, officially ask you?"

He continued eating, but I saw him smile at his plate. "That's up to you, Connor," he said in a low voice without looking up.

My heart and my thoughts were racing. *Okay then. Marriage proposal. Then marriage. Do we get rings? Do I buy them before or after I ... ask ... him ... to ... marry ... me...*

Fuck.

It was finally dawning on me, this conversation we were having. We had already been together for eight years and committed to spending our lives together so it would just be a formality. But, still. Married. On paper, yes, but *still.* Married. That was huge.

But because it was Jamel, I knew it would be okay.

We didn't talk about it again. But I made love to him passionately that night, and Jamel left early for work the next day. I worked the morning, then took the afternoon off to head into Providence and do all that I needed to do. We didn't talk about it at dinner; it was like the conversation never happened. But I wasn't going to let it go. I heard what he said, and he was right. Every major decision regarding our relationship had been Jamel putting things into motion. It was my turn. And I was going to do right by the man that had stood by me all these years.

I waited until he got into bed, then I crawled in after him and laid on my side to face him. He was on his back, but he turned his head to look at me. I stared at him until he slowly turned his whole body to me. He reached his hand out, ran his fingers through the side of my hair and down my arm. I stared into his gray eyes that were so full of love for me. *How could I not want to marry this man?*

"I love you, Jamel," I said.

"I love you too, baby."

My heart was pounding out of my chest. It wasn't like Jamel would say no, but it still made me nervous to do it. I slid off the mattress, knelt down of the bed and reached my hand out. Jamel smiled and sat up, taking my hand. I took a breath, then began.

"Jamel, you've given so much of yourself to me and this relationship. It's solid and amazing because of you. You've never hesitated to show me how you feel about me, about us. Even when I'm feeling vulnerable and insecure and I ask you not to leave me, you never fail to make me feel secure, and assure me that you aren't going anywhere, ever. So I guess this is my way of letting you know that I'm never leaving you. That I love you and want you in my life forever. And I guess the best way to do that is to, you know, give you permission to pull the plug."

Jamel smiled softly and absentmindedly squeezed my hand. He waited patiently for me to continue.

"So. If you're in agreement, I would love to marry you. Do you want to marry me?"

My lover, as usual, did not hesitate. He grabbed my other hand in his, kissed them both, then softly kissed my lips.

"Yes," he said. "I would love to marry you, Connor."

❤

We had two wedding dates. The first was October 17, 2017. We went down to the courthouse in Providence and stood before a judge. On that day, only Afia and Ty were there with us. Then we got matching ring tattoos on our left ring fingers because neither of us wanted actual rings.

But then our mothers found out and raised holy hell: How dare we get married without them? Even though we tried to explain to them it was just a marriage on paper, they would not hear of it. So, we had to plan an actual wedding. Or really, they planned the wedding, and we went along with whatever they wanted to do. My mom told Owen that she was helping her friend Denita plan a wedding for her son and never mentioned who her son was marrying. My sisters went along with it to protect her.

We left everything to them, from the flowers to the cake. The only thing we asked was that it be on the 17th again, our lucky number. So, we got married again, on the same date the following year, October 17, 2018, in his AME church and ordained by the priest from our old Catholic Church. Jamel wore all white with a black trim, and I wore all black with white trim—symbolic of us. Everyone we knew and loved was there. By the time I planted a hot and heavy ten-second kiss on my husband, we both knew our mothers were right. It was the right decision.

We had a reception but left early, leaving our friends and family members there to party, so we could get home to the dogs. We put our foot down at a honeymoon; we both had way too much going on right now, but we'd plan a trip next year, somewhere tropical. We didn't even make love that night; we just laid together in that way we do, with the phoenix tattoo on my back that I got for my 30th birthday laying against his lion claw. He held me tight, and we fell asleep with our dogs in the bed with us.

It was a perfect day.

BOOK CLUB QUESTIONS

1. There are a lot of themes in the Hidden Love Series: LGBTQ and coming out; interracial relationships; military experiences; physical abuse; emotional abuse; conservative Christianity verses progressive Christianity; the gay community and the church; friendships and your chosen family, etc. What theme or themes had the most impact on you and why?
2. The time period is specifically set in between 2009 and 2013. Was this time period relevant to the story?
3. The first three books flowed as one story. Did the author do a good job of organizing the plot and moving it along?
4. Matthew is one of the most hated characters in the series because of his obvious racism and homophobia, but the author describes Matthew's own physical and emotional abuse at the hands of his father, just like Connor. Why do you believe Connor and Matty had two different responses to their father's abuse?

5. Did the Assistant District Attorney have an ulterior motive or was he just doing his job? Explain your reasoning.
6. Did the court hearings—arraignment and trial—come across as authentic to you as the reader? If not, what would have made it more authentic?
7. Pretend you were on the jury. According to the letter of the law, was Connor innocent or guilty?
8. How did you feel about the evolving relationship between Connor and Major Wendel Jones throughout the Hidden Love Series?
9. Would you read a story revolving around Jack and Connor's relationship as teenagers? Why or why not?
10. Were you rooting for Jamel and Connor to get together all along? Why or why not?
11. What do you think will happen next to the main characters?
12. Are you looking forward to Book 4 of the Hidden Love Series, *Deeply Devoted To Him* that will include Jamel's POV? Why or why not?

❤ • ❤ • ❤   AUTHOR BIO: ❤ • ❤ • ❤

Wife, mother, partner, daughter, sister, friend, social worker, life skills coach and part-time erotic romance novelist, Eskay Kabba finds the complexity of human nature and my characters reflect the notion that no one is all good or all bad, but we are all just trying find love in hard places. Eskay pens erotic romance novels that celebrate the LGBTQ community, people of color, and interracial relationships.